BETWEEN FRIENDS

A City Between Compliation

W.R. GINGELL

For Pet, Jin Yeong, Zero, and Athelas.
Thanks for the memories and the sneaky therapy.

TRAINING THE PET

(This story occurs somewhere within the timeframe of book three)

THE HOUSE WAS A MESS. THERE WAS, IN GENERAL, SOME MESS TO it; this time, however, the mess had all the distinct hallmarks of the Pet's influence. The Pet, in fact, had been baiting the vampire, with the predictable result that Jin Yeong had bitten its arm.

"Why can't you train it?" complained Jin Yeong—or some facsimile thereof in Korean. Jin Yeong refused to speak English, and Zero understood him only because Jin Yeong tended to lace the things he wanted understood with copious hints of Between, making it inherently understandable to Zero.

"Thought you wanted blood snacks," said the Pet. "Look, my arm's gone all floppy again. I can't cook with a floppy arm."

"Jin Yeong, stop biting the Pet," said Zero. He didn't smile, and that was more than he'd hoped for.

Jin Yeong said in excuse, "Yes, but *hyeong*, she's so biteable."

"At least I'm not flamin' annoying!" said the Pet.

Zero saw JinYeong bite back a swift answer. Pouting now, the vampire said, "Pet. Good Pet. Give me blood snacks."

"Dunno," said the Pet. "Told you; my arm's gone floppy. How can I clear up in there with a floppy arm?"

JinYeong made an annoyed noise and stalked into the kitchen, rolling his cuffs twice as he went. Zero heard the sound of dishes being cleared, and the Pet grinned its delight at the room.

"I would also like to advocate for further training," said Athelas, the fourth denizen of the house, though he looked more amused than disapproving.

He was not, Zero noticed, sitting in his usual, favourite chair. The Pet had put Athelas' tea and biscuits in a different spot this morning; it was now sitting cross-legged in Athelas' favourite chair itself.

"I don't know," said Zero very deliberately. "It seems to me that there has already been a more than successful level of training achieved."

PET VS VAMPIRE

(This story also occurs somewhere within the timeframe of book three)

THE VAMPIRE WAS HUNGRY. OR WAS HE IRRITATED? HE WASN'T sure.

No, he was feeling oppressed; a gentle, flowery sort of oppression that curled its way around him and weighed him down invisibly.

He had been feeling oppressed for the last week, in fact.

He looked over at the Pet suspiciously, because when something went wrong or mischievous around the house, it was usually the Pet. His look did no good; the Pet was asleep with its brow creased, murmuring "No, no, *no!*" in an increasingly frantic voice.

The vampire sauntered across the room and kicked the Pet's couch as he passed by on the way to his bedroom. The Pet stopped whimpering with a small snort, falling asleep again, and the vampire padded softly upstairs.

The feeling of discomfort was strongest in his bedroom, and he wanted to figure it out before the Pet was awake to watch him in silent sarcasm.

The vampire paced into his room, and there it was again. That intangible sense of oppression.

What was it?

The vampire's nose flared, and as it did, a sudden realisation struck him.

There was an alien scent lingering in the air of his bedroom—or at least, a scent that wasn't itself alien, but shouldn't be where it was. Perhaps the familiarity of it was why it had taken him so long to figure it out.

In his own language, he yelled, "Pet! Pet! Come here!" lacing it with magic to make sure the Pet woke.

The Pet was there a moment later, big eyes blinking at him with unconvincing innocence. "Gunna hurt yourself, yelling like that," it said, in English. Then it grinned at him. "Found something weird, did ya?"

"Why is *his* scent in my room?" the vampire asked coldly.

He asked it in his own language—as he always did. He knew the Pet could understand him; its eyes were dancing. No doubt it had put a drop of the house steward's aftershave somewhere around his room—the wardrobe, by the smell of it.

Despite that, the Pet said, "What? Can't understand you. Speak English."

"Clean it up."

A little louder, as if to a deaf person, the Pet said, "What's that? Can't. Understand. You!"

The vampire pointed into the wardrobe, warning the Pet with the faintest of snarls.

"Oh, did someone spill Athelas' aftershave in your wardrobe?" the Pet asked sympathetically. "What a shame. That musta been annoying you for *so long*."

The vampire grinned. No matter how sarcastic the Pet became, it would clean its mess.

To his surprise, the Pet grinned back at him. "All right, fair cop," it said. "But if I go overtime cleaning up here with soap and water, your dinner's gunna be late."

The vampire's eyes narrowed. They flicked from the Pet and down to his watch, then back to the Pet. There was barely half an hour before dinner time, and he was not the only denizen of the house.

He pursed his lips, but clicked his fingers at the perfumed stain. The lingering scent of aftershave rose from the carpet and dissipated slowly.

"Thanks!" said the Pet, its eyes bright. "See ya at dinner."

It skipped away down the stairs, and the vampire remembered too late—much too late—that tonight was takeaway night.

He opened his mouth to call the Pet back, but it was already long gone, gurgles of laughter tripping down the stairs after it, and the vampire found that he was smiling.

With difficulty, he made his mouth prim again. There was still the faintest scent of aftershave in the air, but he no longer felt oppressed.

"Next time, Pet," said the vampire.

WIDDERSHINS TO DEISEIL

(Yep. Book three again. If you look carefully, you'll know exactly where...)

"Oi."

Detective Tuatu closed his eyes briefly, and opened them again. He knew that voice. A phone call from the girl called Pet was usually trouble.

"What?" he asked cautiously. He already had a plant that seemed to watch him no matter where he was in the room thanks to Pet, and he didn't want anything else off-loaded onto him. "I've got enough house plants and I'm better now."

"Know anything about widdershins?"

"What?"

"You know, widdershins?"

"My grandmother said never to go that way."

"Oh. Whoops."

"Whoops, what?" Detective Tuatu stood involuntarily. Pet was trouble, but she was also human, unlike a lot of his new acquaintanceship, and he had a certain brotherly sort of care where she was concerned. "Where are you?"

"Between a couple of floors, I reckon," she said. "Relax. Sit back down. I'm fine. What else did your grandmother say about widdershins?"

"Never go that way!"

"You said that."

"Go back as soon as possible."

"What else?"

Detective Tuatu found that he was squeezing the phone too tightly, and loosened his white-fingered grip. "Pet, where are you?"

"Told ya. Between floors somewhere. Did your grandma tell you something about how to get out of somewhere when you've gone widdershins?"

He cast about wildly in his mind, trying to think of those long-gone, sunny island days when his grandmother had seemed more mad than sane, but he hadn't cared because he was a kid and she loved him.

Nothing.

He stared at the pot plant, and the pot plant stared back at him; then, dredged from the deepest mires of his memory, a word rose to the surface. "Deiseil!" he said. "She said you have to go deiseil to fix it. You have to look for the sun."

"Don't reckon that's gunna help," she said. "I'm inside."

Detective Tuatu was about to ask again, and with considerably more force, exactly where she was, when it occurred to him to ask instead, "Does it have to be a real sun?"

"Ohhhhh!" said Pet, her deep little voice amused and satisfied. "Ah man, that's clever! Thanks! Catch ya next time!"

She actually hung up on him.

Detective Tuatu called her back, stabbing at the circular numbers on the touch pad of his phone, and when she picked up, he said, "Pet—"

"Don't call me," said Pet's voice. "I'm supposed to be sneaking. I'll bring ya something nice as a thank you later on."

"Don't bring me something!" said the detective, but it was too late. She'd already hung up again. He said accusingly to the pot plant, "*Now* look what you've done."

ZERO SUM GAME

(This one is set between—ha!—books three and four)

ATHELAS SIPPED HIS TEA.

"You owe me," said the Pet. "You flamin' killed me!"

"And yet," said Athelas, "here we are!"

"Doesn't mean you didn't kill me."

Athelas smiled faintly. The Pet was terrier-like in many ways.

"I broke no bargains by killing you," he told her.

"That's rude," the Pet said gloomily. She didn't argue, but that was true to form; the Pet had forgiven him for killing her, and she wouldn't push beyond that forgiveness, even for the answers she so desperately wanted. "Could at least answer a few questions."

She knew he wouldn't do so—he had made it very clear to her that he gave nothing for free.

"Three questions," he said, running a finger along the lip of his teacup briefly. "Nothing owed, nothing given."

"Thought you said it didn't work like that," said the Pet,

shooting him a surprisingly sharp look. "Thought you said it had to be an even exchange."

"Consider this an exception."

"Can I save 'em up?"

"I beg your pardon?"

"Can I save 'em up? Ask 'em another time."

"No."

"Oh. That's a shame."

"You have no questions?" Athelas asked, amused. "How unusual."

"Nah. Got some questions about Zero."

Athelas stifled a sigh. He should have known. He would have to be careful how he answered questions about his lord.

"How come Zero really keeps me here? And don't tell me it's 'cos of my cooking—I won't believe you. I'm pretty sure you could get a fae butler who cooks better."

"I believe that Zero thinks you have hidden depths," said Athelas thoughtfully, for he could only guess, himself. He had had his own reasons for instigating his lord to keep the Pet, but he was quite sure those reasons weren't the same as Zero's reasons for keeping her, though perhaps they overlapped. "You are certainly an oddity, for a human."

"How come you gave me three questions?"

Athelas laughed softly. "Is that one of your questions?"

"Nope," said the Pet, and her little face was sharp and bright. "Just checking something."

"What were you checking?"

"Oi, whose questions are these, mine or yours?"

"Answering a question with a question, Pet?"

"Getting good at this, aren't I?" she said, with a small, deep chuckle.

"A matter of perspective, I suspect. Well?"

"You said not to get fond of Zero, because fae can't be fond of people."

"Quite correct—but not a question."

"Yeah, but you're fae, too."

"Also correct—also not a question."

"Well, what do you do when you find yourself getting fond of someone?"

"I do not," said Athelas, sipping his tea, "get fond of people."

"All right," said the Pet. "You want another cuppa?"

Athelas, for once startled into putting down his teacup, asked, "Are you not going to ask your last question?"

"Nope," said the Pet, perching on the arm of his chair. "Reckon I know the answer to it, anyway. Have a bikkie."

The Pet, thought Athelas, his mind running very swiftly now, acted as though she had gained the information she wanted. That was a dangerous thing, for despite what he had told the Pet, the game was always the same.

In this game, anything the Pet gained was something which Athelas lost, in equal measure. And Athelas couldn't afford to lose anything.

CLOUDY WITH A CHANCE OF DROPBEARS

(This story is firmly in the middle of books five and six, shaking its fist at the rest of the series)

THEY SAY BEHIND IS DANGEROUS AND BETWEEN IS CHANCY—that only the human world with its blind, bumbling occupants is a haven for the Fair Folk. Well, I'm not exactly one of the *fair* folk, and if Australia isn't as dangerous as the most feared parts of Behind, I'll eat my own wooden leg.

Properly speaking, there's Australia Behind and Australia Between, but when it comes to Behind and Between, it's nearly the same thing no matter where in the human world it joins up. Go anywhere Behind and it's the same Behind; it's all fae and vampires and selkies, that sort of thing. A few of us leprechauns, too. Behind is the place the human world doesn't know exists. Even Between isn't too different; it's just the way it looks that's different—depending on if you know *how* to look, if you get my drift.

It's not the same when it comes to travelling between places in the human world. I've been in civilized places like England and

Canada, and it's a world away from the nightmare land of red heat and deadly animals they call Australia. They don't let you into Australia from Behind until you've passed your survival fitness exam, which should tell you something.

I hadn't passed that exam. I didn't want to pass that exam. I would have gladly spent the rest of my life in a cubicle safely Behind the human world. And yet here I was, stuck headfirst in a tree on the human-world side of Australia, with *my* behind exposed to the elements and the dull thud of dropbears hitting the ground around me.

Let me explain. I wasn't planning on going to Australia that day —that day or ever. I'm a leprechaun, the closest thing you can get to a living calculator, and until that day I was perfectly happy crunching numbers in my cubicle. For us, it's about the closest thing you can get to pure happiness unless you own your own private supply of gold coins to count every day. That rainbow with the promised gold at the end of it—that's what a cubicle and something to count means to a leprechaun.

I was ready for a big day. My wooden leg was hurting when I got up, and that means a day of either finding or losing huge amounts of money. And if you're going to tell me a wooden leg can't hurt, you can kick off out of here any time, because mine always hurts when there's going to be big money, so there. I just didn't know whether it was going to be a finding or losing day. Finding or losing doesn't matter to me, mind you—I just find out where the money's gone. If it was my money, it would matter a lot more; but it's not, and it doesn't.

I sat down in my chair at the office in an almost jovial frame of mind. I startled the coffee boy by grinning at him, scaring him so much that he spilled the coffee and had to go back for more. Served him right, lanky-legged little lollygagger that he was. Grinning a bit wider, I logged onto my work portal and rubbed my hands together to see the first case waiting for me.

"Never failed me yet!" I declared, slapping my wooden leg. The first case that popped up on my portal was the one I'd been working off and on for the last few months—something from a group called Allied Traders. They were a group that worked across Between to trade with the human world (coffee and other stuff that the humans do better than Behind) and on paper, things almost looked kosher. *Almost.*

Then you went a bit deeper and found that the things you should have found a bit deeper weren't there. Things like human resources—Allied Traders had warehouses on this side and the human side of Between for any resources from the human world— weren't in the warehouse they were meant to be in. Actually, there wasn't anything in the warehouses at all except a very sleepy fae guard once you got past the magical defences. Good thing leprechauns are so good at getting past anything magic, isn't it?

That's what I thought, anyway, sitting there and grinning at my portal. I'd taken a trip yesterday, and last night I'd clued in my supervisor. If I did things right for the next twenty years or so, maybe I'd get promoted up the chain for this.

I went and got my own coffee before the coffee boy got back, eager to sniff out more payments that had a suspicious lack of product to go with them. I put the mug down on my desk and settled myself to sit down, but something sharp and hot seared my leg where my Behind Identify Card should be. I yelped and pinched it out of my pocket. Behind magic is the good stuff, but there's nothing that melts faster than an Identify Card, magic or no magic. Something about magic and the newer human manufactured substances doesn't blend well.

Now that I looked at the card, too, it was a lot blacker than it should be. Well, parts of it were blacker than they should be, and it was still hot in my fingers, too. Was it *burnt*?

I squinted down at it, irritated to find that my glasses weren't around my neck, and reached for the desk where the missing glasses should have been.

My desk wasn't there. Actually, the office wasn't there. No

wonder the ground was so squishy beneath my peg—it was real grass, not the magic-fake they put in Behind offices.

Great. Someone had relocated the office without telling me. I'd send off a pretty strong message as soon as I found where those goons in Location had parked it this time. I'm as security-conscious as the next leprechaun, but there was no way we'd been found so soon after the last move. No way I should have been left behind, either.

I looked down at my Identify card again, and it looked a bit red in the middle. Red in the middle, and if I squinted at it just right, there were words making a black scrawl in the centre of the red bit.

Kill the kid and you can come back, it said.

I snuffled a dry laugh down at it. Somebody was having a laugh. It was a bit stupid, though; *kid* was the word used for human children, and who was going to find a kid Behind? I looked a bit closer at the words, and a sticky breeze swept across my forearms, raising goosebumps in spite of its warmth. That wasn't just red behind the writing. It was Red. If somebody was having a laugh, *why was my Identify Card marked Red for Deport?* Deportation Red meant tried, executed, and deported. No return to Behind.

That was stupid. Someone *had* to be having a laugh. I was still Behind...wasn't I? But where in Behind was I? I looked around me, dazedly taking in the dark green foliage of trees and the playground, and the half tree that someone had turned into a house—wait. The *playground?* Fae don't have playgrounds. And why was the heat so heavy today? Where in Behind had access to this kind of muggy heat? Muggy...*muggy* heat? There's no muggy heat Behind; too many weather mages.

"No," I said numbly, sweat springing to my brow. "Because that means I'm—that means I'm in the *human* world."

Red for Deport. I was in the human world.

"What did *I* do?" I demanded of the hollowed-out tree house, my voice high and panicked. "I paid my taxes. *Found* taxes. Gave my leg for the Fae Corp in the Third war!"

I sat down in the grass and buried my head in my hands. This was bad. The worst. I couldn't survive in the human world. I wasn't trained. I wasn't ready. I didn't even have a job! Who would keep me in gold if I had no job? And the humans—how was I supposed to communicate with them? I didn't even know if you *could* communicate with them; it was bad enough trying to communicate with the milk cows that were brought over from the human world when ours died out.

Something bit me beneath my trousers, and if the air around me was a muggy heat, this was a fiery heat. I yelled and shot to my feet, slapping at the spot, and pinched whatever the heck it was through the trousers and out into the open. It was an ant, squirming and dying, its broken legs flailing at me. With my Sight I could see the poison on its pincers, even if my normal sight wasn't good enough to properly make out the pincers, and when I looked back down at my leg, horrified, I could see the same poison beginning to course through my veins from the point of the bite.

But...but it was so *small*. How could it be so deadly?

I threw the ant away from me and slapped my hand back over the bite, drawing out the poison in the same way I'd drawn out the ant. It came out reluctantly, as fast-spreading as it had been in my blood. I didn't know if my legs were weak because of the poison, or the fact that I'd almost left it too late to treat comfortably. What was this place? What place had such tiny, deadly animals?

And why was it so skin-meltingly *hot*, for all that was gold?

I didn't dare to sit on the ground again. At home the grass was green and plump and cool, free from murderous insects and good for recharging; here, now, I could see that it was teeming with deadly life. Gold only knew what kind of other venomous insects were waiting to kill me. There was a nice, sunny spot on the metal play equipment; it was bright and sunny as well, painted in yellow and orange, and I felt that at least there was a shining spot to the day thus far.

I breathed out a sigh of relief, hopeful of soaking up a little energy from the sun, and sank down on the metal square.

It *burnt*.

For the second time in five minutes, I leaped to my feet with a howl, clutching my rear. Was it silver? Who makes human playgrounds out of silver? But there was no debilitating spread of *malaise*, no nausea; just a pained kind of after-burn that faded slowly but left me disinclined to sit down again right away.

It was just hot. So *gold-fired* hot from the sun that it had burned me to sit down on it.

I whimpered a bit. I didn't really care where I was anymore; I just wanted to go back home. I picked a spot in the shady brown instead of the sunny brown, and sat down—this time very carefully—on something wooden and duck-shaped that wobbled beneath me but didn't burn me. A sensation of coolness soothed my burnt backside, but I couldn't feel anything energetic in the grass beneath my feet.

I groaned into my hands. "Where can I even *recharge* in this place?"

"Athelas likes to use the waterfall in Snug," said a voice. "Zero prefers the sea. But if you want to use something nearby, there's always the Huon river."

I looked up wildly. It was a kid. Standing there in front of me with its hands in its pockets. I didn't know if it was male or female —you can't tell with humans; they're all so ugly, and they don't smell of anything. At least with Behinders you can tell who's male and who's female by smell. I didn't know how long it had been there, either.

I stared at it while the sweat trickled down my temple and made a prickling line right to my collar.

Kill the kid and you can come back. That's what the writing on my card said. Well, this was the only kid in the area; long-legged and long-haired, it had a hopeful sort of expression to its face. I mean, it was still ugly, but it was ugly in a nice sort of way. It looked like you could pat it on the head without being bitten. Not that I could reach, but still.

"You appeared out of nowhere," it said to me. It sounded thoughtful but not surprised. "I don't know what kind you are."

I glared at it. It knew a bit too much for a human, didn't it? Or was it just confused? I said, "Kind? What do you mean?"

"You know—Behindkind." It tilted its head. "I know you are one, just can't tell what kind. You're not tall enough for fae or pouty enough to be a vampire. Are you a troll?"

"Who do you think you're calling a troll!" I demanded, sitting up straight in outrage. The wooden duck wobbled and threatened to dump me in the brown, crackly grass.

"Oh, sorry," it said. "Didn't mean to offend you. I know a troll and she's really nice."

"That's because they're eager-to-please little nubkinses!" I snarled, clinging with both hands to the wobbling duck's wooden handles. "They should just accept that they're ugly and no one loves them."

"Oh," said the kid. It didn't try to say anything else—just sat there as if it was waiting for me to notice something.

I ignored it. "Red for Deport," I muttered to myself. "Who has that clout and who would do it? Who am I? Just a little government lep' looking for his next pay stream. No need to mark me Red for Deport, was there? Who's the sorry beetle that sent me off into the human world without a trial?"

"I don't know about that," said the kid, "but I don't think we're actually in the human world."

"'Course we are," I said, without paying too much attention. "Where else would we be? You're a human. The place *feels* human— gives me a nasty shiver."

"Ye-es," said the kid uneasily. "But—"

"And I'm a leprechaun. Don't go calling me a troll."

That distracted it. "Oh. There are leprechauns Behind! What's your name?"

"Five-Four-One."

The kid giggled. "Really?"

I scowled at it. "That's my batch number. What else would it be? Wipe that smirk off your face."

"Sorry," the kid said, but it was still grinning. "But around here there's a saying that goes *I'd rather have a number than a name like that*, and you've already got a number, so—!"

Maybe this one wasn't as intelligent as I'd thought it was. At least it wasn't as stupid as the human cows had been.

It was clever enough to notice my scowl growing. It managed to smother its grin a bit, and asked, "Why are you here, anyway?"

"Curious, aren't you?" I said sourly. I sneaked a peek at my card, but it was still red and black, the writing still jumping out at me. *Kill the kid and you can come back*. That was all well and good, but why should I? Who was this mysterious kidnapper to tell me to kill someone for them? Even a human kid. That's the sort of thing I don't approve of.

But if I didn't, how would I get home? I couldn't live here. I needed my gold. I needed a place to recharge. Without those things, I would die even sooner than a human in this part of the world.

I looked at the kid meditatively, which seemed to make it nervous. "What?" it asked.

"You," I said. "What are you doing here?"

"Same as you," it said, a bit more cheerfully.

"What?" Did it have a card, too? Death matches were illegal Behind, but the governing powers could be stretchy when it came to applying Behind laws to Behindkind in the human world.

"I just appeared, like you," said the kid. "Well, I think so, anyway. Right in the middle of making dinner, too. They're gonna be annoyed—'s'pecially Jin Yeong. Stuff always happens when I'm cooking his choice."

"Cooking?" I glared at it. "What the everlasting gold are you chuntering about? Nobody cares about whether or not your dinner gets cooked."

"Yeah, but that's the thing," the kid argued. "Jin Yeong cares, and that means he's gonna be stroppy as all heck when he finds me."

"I don't care if Jin Yeong is stroppy as all heck!" I snapped. I didn't even know what *stroppy as all heck* meant. "What is this place, and why have you dragged me here? You've no business marking me Red for Deport!"

The kid looked indignant. "I just *said*! I didn't have anything to do with it; I was in the kitchen and then I was here. I mean, I think I know where I am, but when I tried to start walking home, I couldn't get out."

"Out?"

"Yeah. It's weird; I can usually get in and out of Between without any problems, but whenever I try to walk past the picnic table to go home, I find myself walking back past the treehouse again."

"This isn't Between," I said, very slowly and loudly. "It's the human world." For all that was gold! It was a human! Why didn't it know its own world?

The kid looked like it was trying not to grin again. "Yeah," it said. "But you try walking out and see how you go."

I didn't like the way it was grinning, but I had to try now. I stumped toward the picnic table, my wooden leg sinking too deeply into the brown grass, and found myself walking past the treehouse instead.

"Flamin' weird, isn't it?" said the kid, in a chummy sort of way. "What d'you reckon's happened?"

I glared at it. Was it stupid or senseless? No one in their right mind should be that comfortable and trusting when they had been thrown into a closed circle with someone who, for all they knew, could have been ordered to kill them.

"Maybe we should see if we can get over it," the kid suggested. "I reckon its fae magic, and fae don't think about loopholes as much as I thought they would. Well, not when it comes to humans, anyway. They think we're as dumb as cows over here, so they don't usually make things too hard for us."

I coughed and tapped my wooden leg against the ground. "That right?"

The kid grinned again. "Yeah. Oi. If you give me a leg up, I reckon I can climb over the top of whatever spell they're using."

"A *leg up?*" Was that meant to be a joke?

"Or I'll give you one, if you like, but I reckon I might be lighter than you."

Oh. It wanted a *boost*. "I can get you to the first branch of that tree," I said. On the side that wasn't road and gravel, the trees surrounded the playground and overhung it; at least one of those branches should be caught in the same bubble as us.

And if the kid was right—who was I kidding? Of course it was right. There's nothing so snooty and self-confident as an intelligent fae. And they *all* think they're intelligent.

"Should I climb on your shoulders, or—"

"No!"

"Oh. Well, how am I going to—"

"Turn arou—" I snapped, slapping at the containment spell to see exactly where it was. And that was as far as I got. Something raw and strong and magical threw me across the playground the instant I touched fae magic. I hit the tree house, though it felt more like the tree house hit me, and for a very long, dusty, grassy time, I whimpered up at the sky.

There was the sound of running footsteps, and a voice yelled, "Five! Five, are you okay?"

I considered whimpering again, but the kid might have heard me. "No, I'm not okay!"

"Right," said the kid. Its face appeared above me, then wiry arms tugged at me until I could sit up. "Yeah. Um, can you stand up?"

"No!" I snarled, and stood up a bit hazily. I'd been winded, and that was as bad as it was, but there was no way I was going to say that after the fuss I'd made. "If I've broken anything—!"

The kid was grinning again. Guess I'd underestimated how much it knew about injuries. "Look on the bright side," it said. "At least your peg leg isn't broken."

"With all this gold-perishing sunlight there's no other way to look at things," I grumbled.

"Yeah, the hole in the ozone layer is right above us," the kid said cheerfully. "Wanna try again?"

"No!" There was a pause before I said grudgingly, "Yes. But I have to pee first. Another impact like that and the grass'll think the rains have come to this gold-perishingly barren place."

There was a barely stifled laugh from the kid, but it said, "Wouldn't do that f'I were you."

"What? Why can't I pee?"

"It's not that you can't," the kid said, "but there was a redback on the toilet seat in the loo yesterday, and I don't know where it went."

"What's a redback?"

"Spider. Pretty deadly."

"Either it's deadly or it isn't."

The kid considered that. "Then I s'pose it depends on how quickly you get to the hospital, and if they have the stuff to treat it."

"I don't have to sit."

"I didn't say it lives under the loo seat; that's just where I saw it last. I was moving pretty quick then, so I didn't see where it went after that. And I think it got touched by Between a bit, so it might be bigger than usual."

"Is *everything* here trying to kill me?"

"Not everything," said the kid. Its eyes, which had been looking around curiously at something I hadn't seen, widened. "Oh. But *those* might be."

There were so many trees out there, all green and brown from the heat, that I didn't see the perishers until the kid pointed them out. About four or five *very big* bears surrounded the playground from every direction that contained trees, their greyish pelts blending into the branches they clung to with long, sharp claws, their eyes black and glittering in the shadowy foliage. They were each the size of a decently grown polar bear, and as they made their way toward us through the branches, the tree branches shook as if in an impossibly high wind.

"What are those? *What are those!?*" My voice cracked. I'm not proud of it, but that's what happened.

"I think they're dropbears," the kid said thoughtfully. "It's weird. They shouldn't exist."

"Dropbears?" I said feebly. "What are dropbears?"

Whatever else they were, they were definitely Between creatures —chimeras made of possibility, magic, and malice.

"Kind of like *really* mean, really big koalas," the kid said. It was looking less thoughtful and more alarmed as the dropbears shuddered closer through the trees. "They drop from trees and tear you to bloody pieces. They weren't—I mean, they don't exist. They're a thing that was made up for TV ads. They're not a thing that properly comes from Between."

I squeezed my eyes shut and hoped desperately that when I opened them, the dropbears would have disappeared. They hadn't.

I said, "They do now."

But wait. We weren't Between—we were firmly in the human world. How in the woody green were Between-magicked dropbears approaching from *the human world?*

"How?" I panted, mopping more sweat from my brow than I'd thought possible for my body to contain in its entirety. "We're not Between! They shouldn't be here!"

"Yeah," said the kid. "That's what I thought. That's why I said we're Between, even though it doesn't feel quite the same. Zero isn't here, so I thought I'd wait and see what happened, but then you arrived so I s'pose we should try to do something about it."

"These things have been there all along!?"

"Mostly," the kid said. "They didn't start coming closer until you started flying around, though."

"*I wasn't flying around!* I was suffering blowback from your stupid—"

"I don't think you can really blame that on me," the kid said seriously. "It was the containment thingie. I'm not magical or anything."

"It's *Other*. You say you're *not Other*."

"Yeah. So you can't blame that on me, can you?"

"Well, it was your idea!" I said nastily. "I don't go around getting close to Other spells for no reason. I suppose you think I just threw myself in the air for the fun of it!"

"I thought it was pretty funny," the kid muttered, but when I snarled "*What?*" at it, it cleared its throat and tried to look innocent. "Nothing."

"See how funny you find it all when the dropbears get to us," I told it.

"Wait, though," said the kid uncertainly. "The spell should stop them too, shouldn't it?"

"Wouldn't count on it," I said sourly. Of all the ways to go! I'd survived the 3rd war, even if my right leg hadn't, and now I was about to be sent off by a pack of dropbears. Mind you, the dropbears were in the trees; they were still approaching, but it wasn't too much of a stretch to think they might not be clever enough to try and go over the spell.

Only they never did drop from the trees; they kept lumbering through the foliage in a storm of shaking until they were well past the tree we'd been trying to boost each other into.

"Oh," said the kid. "Reckon they figured out the spell, too."

"Right."

"We should try to get out again," said the kid.

It was clearer toward the front of the playground that faced the road, so we legged it toward that part. There was only one tree there, but before we got to its trunk the spell set us hurrying back toward the treehouse again.

"Reckon the treehouse is the centre of the spell," the kid panted, when we'd righted ourselves again. "Look, we can reach that branch, though. You ready to try again?"

I wasn't, but I said, "Right," anyway. What else could we do?

"Maybe I should try boosting you this time," the kid said.

"Let's do that." I wouldn't have suggested it myself because I'm not a coward, but since it had suggested the idea itself... "That'll work."

And it worked. Oh boy, did it work. The idea had been to give me a gentle boost and circumvent whatever gold-perished magic some Behindkind had put on the inside of the spell.

It gave me a boost, all right. We couldn't make sure exactly where the Behindkind magic was without touching it, but it sure knew where we were. The kid boosted, I hit the magic, and with that magic behind it, the boost sent me sailing further into the air than the first jolt had done. I flew back over the playground, grass and trees a brown-and-green blur around me. There was a bigger blur of brown for just long enough for me to realise that I was going to hit the tree house headfirst this time, then I was stuck like a cork in a bottle.

And there I was, somewhere in Australia, human-world side, head and shoulders in a tree with my rear exposed to the elements and the dropbears thudding to the grass all around me.

"Better wriggle!" yelled the kid. "They're in!"

I wriggled. I wriggled harder than I'd done since I was hatched, a crawling feeling running up and down the leg I didn't have any more, warning that my other leg was about to be bitten off. A scratching lower in the tree house made me stop short, unsure whether it was safer in or out, but then the kid popped up from a small hole in the floor and grabbed my arms.

There was another brief moment where I felt like a cork in a bottle before I exploded inward. The kid yelped as I head-butted its stomach but hauled me to my feet without retaliating.

"Couldn't wedge the door shut," it gasped. "It's too small for them to get in that way, anyway. Wouldn't count on the treehouse being strong enough to stop 'em if they really want us, though."

I poked my head out of the round window for another look at the dropbears. "They want us," I said grimly. All five of them were sniffing around the base of the treehouse. They didn't look too bright, but they didn't have to be to get us.

"I reckon it's a trap," the kid said. "They were out there, but they didn't get interested until you got here."

"It's not a trap," I said. "It's insurance."

"Insurance for what?"

"Mind your own business."

"It *is* my business! They want to eat me! Well, I suppose it's you they want to eat, actually, but I don't think they'll stop at you."

"No, it's you they want," I said, without thinking.

"I don't mean to be rude," said the kid, "but that doesn't make much sense. They only tried to come in after you got here."

"It can't be me they're after," I said. "I've been given a task to do, and I can't do it if I'm dead."

"Then what am I here for?"

"To die," I said, and it wasn't wrong.

"I wonder if Zero and Athelas know about this?" the kid said.

It looked pretty comfortable for someone who was about to be eaten by dropbears. Was it expecting me to do something, or was it still waiting for that *Zero* it kept talking about? Trustful didn't even cover this kid.

"We came here a couple days ago because the locals have been hearing weird stuff and seeing lights at night—that sort of thing."

"So I'm not the first to arrive here," I said. I hadn't meant to say it aloud, but there was something about the kid's trustful face that made it easy to talk more than I should. "There have been other Behindkind sent here."

"Yeah, that's what I reckon. And people have been disappearing."

"Humans disappearing?"

The kid nodded. "Yeah. A fair few of 'em, too. Locals, tourists, seasonal workers; doesn't seem to matter who. I reckon the dropbears must have been getting 'em, but why are there dropbears here?"

Humans disappearing in a particular spot? Now that was a pattern I was familiar with, and it was a pattern that didn't involve dropbears. The dropbears were part of something else altogether, but *this*—this place was a human resources source. Not human-made or human-sourced resources like coffee. *Human* resources. A stock supply of humans.

And that meant that Allied Traders was a human stock mill. Someone knew exactly what case had landed on my table that morning, and had made sure I was somewhere a bit too hot to handle.

I grinned. "Now I'm getting somewhere!" I said, satisfaction thick in my voice. It's not like a human stock mill is *illegal*, so to speak. But there are some very specific rules about how the humans can be used, consent, and the safe disposal of them once they're through their indentures. Behind likes to stay a secret.

"What?" asked the kid, its voice quick and indignant. "What did you just figure out?"

"I know why your humans have been disappearing." Now, just how much could I tell it without it figuring out I'd been sent to kill it? "Someone Behind is stealing humans to sell."

"We'll see about that!" said the kid, with a martial light to its eyes. "Just *wait* until I tell Zero about this! Someone is going to be really sorry!"

"No one is going to be sorry," I snapped, "except us! They're going to get away scott free because we're going to die. There are still dropbears out there and we're still in here. They only have to wait. Or break the tree down."

The kid made a *piffle* kind of noise, which was annoying because this wasn't the situation in which anyone should be making a *piffle* noise.

"We're properly Between now," it said. It was grinning; a tough, sideways sort of grin that was directly at odds with the usual trustful look to its face. "The dropbears brought it with them; can't you feel it?"

I scowled at it, because now that it had said so, I *could* sense it. "What's it to you whether we're Between, Behind, or human world?"

"That's the thing." It was still grinning. "Between likes me."

"It *likes*—Between doesn't like people."

"Yeah, well, I can do stuff here."

That settled it; the kid was wrong in the head. Humans couldn't access Between, and they certainly couldn't *do* things Between.

"Don't believe me?"

"Nope," I said, and looked out the window again. One of the dropbears slapped a paw against the tree house and the whole thing shuddered, us with it.

"Okay," said the kid, and pulled a sword out of thin air. No, it was an umbrella that looked like a sword. And now it looked like a sword again.

I blinked hard. It was a sword, but it hadn't always been a sword —or rather, here in the human world it was just the tattered remains of an old umbrella that someone had left in the treehouse on a rainy day. Behind, it had always been a sword. Between, depending on how you saw it, it could be a sword, or it could be an umbrella.

I was definitely having trouble seeing. "Gold perish it!" I snarled. "Who taught you how to do that?"

"JinYeong," said the kid, admiring the sword. It looked pretty pleased with itself, and I didn't much blame it; pulling something out of Between is meant to be impossible for a human. Even for a Behinder, pulling a sword Between isn't the easiest thing in the world. "But Zero was the one who showed me how to see it properly. I've been practising pretty hard lately. Lucky, isn't it?"

"Lucky," I said, with a dry throat.

"Want something?"

"Yeah."

The kid looked around doubtfully. There wasn't a lot to choose from in the tree house; the umbrella was the biggest, sharpest thing in there. Apart from that, there were crumpled little canisters of what looked like thin metal, a few woolly bits of string, something whippy and wooden that could have been for supporting plants, and an assortment of sharp little things that were a mix of glass, metal, and wood.

The kid didn't look worried. "You have this one," it said, passing me the sword.

Kill the kid, said the words burned across my mind, *and you can come back.*

"I don't want it!" I snapped. "Gold perish it, do I look like my arms are long enough for that thing?"

"And there's your leg," the kid said. It was a bit pinker than it had been, though I wasn't sure why. "I didn't think about that. Sorry. How are you at archery?"

"All right," I said, hunching my shoulders. "And I'll thank you to remember that I can still cut a pretty pace with my peg leg!"

"Oh good!" the kid said, and picked up the whippy piece of wood and the longest piece of string. By the time the light of the window fell on them, they weren't plain wood and string any longer; they were a neat little recurve bow and bowstring. "Can you string it? I can't ever get them to bend back enough."

I took it and strung it in two seconds flat. I might have been trying to prove my mettle, but it was a good thing; the whole tree house shook again a moment after I was done. The kid, who was reaching out to snap off old, dried twigs from the outside of the treehouse, nearly fell out the window. I grabbed it by the belt-loops—why did I do that? I didn't have to do that—and after a furious bout of wriggling it came back in, brandishing six arrows at me.

"Enough?"

"Maybe," I said. That left me one bad shot, which in normal circumstances would be enough. This wasn't normal circumstances—but then, nothing in war was ever normal, either, and I'd survived that. "Not if they get in here first."

"Yeah, that's what I thought," said the kid. "You all right by yourself?"

"What?"

"Don't want to waste the sword."

"Do you know how to use it?"

"A bit," said the kid. "Ish. Zero hasn't finished my training yet, and I usually have a couple of lighter ones instead of a big one."

"If you can't string a recurve, you can't hack down that lot with a sword," I said. It had been a while since I'd seen combat, but I still knew that much.

"Just as well you're gonna be up here shooting them, then, isn't it?"

"What?"

"Just make sure you shoot all of 'em so I don't have to do too much work." This time, it sounded like the kid was trying to be cheerful. "I mean, someone's gotta get 'em away from the base; it's not like you can shoot them at this angle. And maybe Zero will come soon. I don't *think* he'll leave me here."

"No use thinking about someone who isn't here," I said. "We're alone until we kill those bears and get over the spell."

"If I get 'em away from the base, reckon you've got a good shot?"

"Get 'em away from the base of the tree and I'll shoot every gold-perishing mother's son of 'em," I said grimly. The kid was right: close range was good, but that angle was too tight.

"All right," said the kid, and vanished.

"Green and gold!" I swore. I hadn't expected it to go that

quickly. I'd expected a bit more hesitation, a bit more whining—maybe a few tears.

I poked my head out the window just in time to see the kid streak from the door, right between two of the dropbears. It was howling at the top of its lungs, which surprised the dropbears so much that they just stood where they were for a moment before they lunged into the chase.

The kid was quick on its feet, I'll give it that. It wasn't even trying to fight; it was just running around yelling, waving its sword. I grinned a bit before I realised what I was doing and scowled instead. The dropbears lumbered after the kid, and I saw my lines clearing up. I edged the bow through the window, no longer afraid to have it knocked out of my hands by a high-swiping dropbear, and shuffled my upper body after it.

Just in time, too. They were in range, and at just the right angle. I lifted the bow—hesitated for a fraction of a second. *Kill the kid and you can come back.* The kid was still running in circles, but it couldn't do that for too long in this kind of heat. I didn't even have to kill it. All I had to do was wait, and the dropbears would do the job. It wasn't like the kid could make it back into the tree house now.

It was just a fraction of a second's hesitation, but in that time, one of them reached out faster than the kid could run and slapped it into the ground. I didn't hesitate again. My bow came up and I shot—twice at the one hanging over the kid, then at the next, then again, and again. The kid scrambled to its feet, bloody and staggering, and waved at me.

I nocked the last arrow and roared, *"Get down!"*

The kid dropped right to its stomach—who had trained it to do that?—and I snatched back the string on my last shot. I was too quick; my elbow hit the side of the tree house and the shot went wide. Flat on its stomach, the kid grimaced. It looked back at the dropbear and then over at its sword. There was no way it would make it to the sword before the dropbear got to it.

What else could I throw? What else was there to throw? The

kid was going to die, and then I could go home, but what else was there to throw?

I furiously unscrewed my peg leg and hurled it at the kid. Stupid trustful little thing, it was still looking up at me. It caught the peg leg in its right hand and curled around in the same movement to flick it in the dropbear's face. The peg leg flickered, grew, shrank again—and hit the dropbear between the eyes. It bounced off, but before it hit the ground the kid was sprinting toward the treehouse.

What in the green and gold did that kid just do to my peg leg? And why didn't it hold?

"Shove over!" said the kid's voice.

I shoved over. It climbed through the hole in the floor, panting, and waved a crooked twig at me.

"Got another one!"

"What do you expect me to hit with this?" I grumbled. The stick had been crooked, and as an arrow, it was still crooked. "Clean your face up."

The kid swiped one hand below its nose, smearing blood. "It's not broken," it said cheerfully. "Reckon your leg is toast, though. Sorry about that. I tried to make it be something else, but it was *really* sure about being a peg leg."

"It was a good leg," I said glumly. The dropbear was out there gnawing on it, stupid beast. "You've got a black eye."

"I know. I can feel it swelling. What are we going to do about that last one? Can you shoot it through the window?"

"Help me down to the door at the bottom," I said. We were probably dead if I missed, anyway; at least out there we were closer to other sticks that might turn into better arrows. "I don't want to try shooting this thing out of the window."

"Yeah," said the kid, wriggling down through the hole in the floor first. It took the bow and arrow from me, then grabbed my whole leg as it came down and steadied my drop to the floor. A bit of training and this kid might make a good officer's boy. "We want to give you the best chance."

"Best chance, my eye!" I grumbled, steadying my half leg on the kid's bent knee. "Just get ready to run for another stick before the dropbear gets to us."

Then I took careful aim, steadied my wrist, and shot.

I missed, of course. The arrow was crooked, for all that's green and gold! But it hit the confinement spell across the playground, and where a straight arrow might have careened sideways due to the spell, this one turned sideways of its own accord for a bare instant before the spell pinged it back across the playground at twice the speed and a terrifying accuracy.

It went through the dropbear's head so fast that the bear probably never felt it. Something thunked into the treehouse with a bloody *smack!* and the bear collapsed into the brown grass, spilling blood.

"Flaming heck!" said the kid.

We stared at the dead bear in silence for a few minutes. I was ruminating on the certainty that I would never again in my life make a shot like that, whether or not there was a 4th War. The kid must have been thinking of something else, because soon it said unexpectedly, "Oi. What happened to your pants?"

I clutched at the back of my trousers. "What do you mean, what happened to my pants?"

"Not there," it said. "The pocket."

My hand slapped the charred bit of cloth that should have been my pocket, and something black and rectangular came away in my hand, shedding tendrils of fabric that floated away on the hot air.

My card. My card was black as ink—black as hopeless death. Now it wasn't just Red for Deportment, it was No Return Whatsoever and Kill on Sight.

I looked down at it, and the kid looked down at it.

"What's that mean?" it asked. "That doesn't look good."

"Nothing," I said. I flicked the card away into the corpse-filled playground and it fluttered for a moment like black ash before it disintegrated. "Don't need it any more, that's all."

"Hang on," the kid said. Its brow was furrowed. "Black...Athelas said something about black-carding a Behindkind—hang on! They're going to kill you?"

"D'like to see 'em try," I muttered. "I've still got one more leg."

"That thing you said you had to do," the kid said unexpectedly. "The errand—it was to kill me, wasn't it?"

"What?"

"You were meant to kill me, weren't you?"

"What—how did you know?"

"Makes sense," the kid said, shrugging. It wandered toward the most freshly dead dropbear and prodded it with one foot. "You remember I said people have been disappearing here and around Tassie?"

"I remember." I didn't look at the kid; for a ridiculous reason I couldn't pinpoint, I felt ashamed. Maybe it was because of how often I'd actually thought about killing it.

"Yeah, well some of 'em came back. Dead. None of the dead ones disappeared around here, but they all came back here when they were dead. And then I was pulled here, and there you were, and the dropbears...so... Do they always send you?"

"What? No, they don't always send me! I'm just a pay-cheque lep'! I haven't drawn bow for twenty years, since the last war!"

"Oh." The kid seemed to accept that, which irritated me. Why was it still so trusting? "Then that was some flaming good shooting."

"Stop trusting people so quickly!" I snapped at it. "That's how you end up dying!"

"I've got good instincts about people," said the kid blithely. "So your card is black because you didn't kill me?"

I shrugged. "Never did learn to do what I was told. I found something I shouldn't have found, and someone sent me here because they wanted to make sure I didn't bring it up somewhere inconvenient."

"Oh," it said. Then, unexpectedly, "Want your leg back? It's a bit chewed up, but it'll still work."

It brandished the mutilated peg leg at me—when did it pick that up?—and a gobbet of dropbear spit smacked into brown dirt.

A rush of affection coursed through me. That was a good leg, that was. Lasted through the second half of a war and a dropbear attack. I'd polish up those bite marks nice and shiny and it'd be just as good as new.

"Go on, then," I said.

The kid cheerfully tried to screw my mutilated wooden leg back on—all right for *it* to be cheerful, *it* was only sporting a black eye and bloody nose; no one was going to kill *it* on sight—and promptly knocked me over again.

I glared at it and tried to get up, but something bigger sent me flying head-over-heels with one blow. When I managed to unscramble my limbs and my brains, there were three much larger figures between me and the kid. It wasn't until I was upright that I realized who they were, and then I wished I'd stayed on the ground.

I knew them all.

Massive, silver, and icily furious, that one in the centre was Lord Sero, heir to half the Behind world. Zero. The kid had said *Zero*. If the kid's *Zero* was Lord Sero, then—then that Athelas it'd spoken of—

My stomach dropped even further. At Lord Sero's left hand was Athelas, steward to Lord Sero—genteel, pleasant, and smiling politely. And if you don't know better than to trust that, there's no hope for you. On Lord Sero's right was *that vampire*. Not everyone knows about him; I guess I'm just lucky. I'd never met him before—though I'd seen his tracks—didn't want to meet him now. He was looking at me like he was curious about how long it would take to drain the blood from someone of my size as opposed to someone of a more average height.

All three of them. All three of them together.

I was going to die.

Great. Twice in one day. If it came right down to a choice between Lord Sero and dropbears, I would have picked the dropbears. At least they were stupid enough to go for a wooden leg.

I didn't even have time to blink before Lord Sero had me by the throat. I gaped up at him, completely out of words. What could I say? I didn't know what I'd done wrong. If he was angry at me for saving the kid, then why was he standing between me and it? If he was trying to protect it, why was he scruffing me?

So I just sort of choked at him for a moment or two until he said, in icy, fragmented words, "*What*. Are you doing. With. My. *Pet?*"

I choked at him again. This time, it could have sounded like, "*What?*"

"*Ah, baegopa!*" sighed the vampire, around Lord Sero's shoulder. I didn't know what he meant by the words, but the cold, sharp-edged grin he shot me was pretty clear. If Lord Sero didn't choke me to death, the vampire would drain me.

"Oi!" yelled a voice. I had the feeling it had been yelling for a while, but do excuse me if I was more concerned with the vampire and the fae. "Let go of him!"

Lord Sero turned, taking me with him. The vampire did too, still showing that half, tooth-edged, and utterly humourless grin, and we all stared at the kid. It stared right back at us, bloody, defiant, and ready to die. It looked so small and helpless.

Did that little human thing *really* just raise its voice at the Lord Sero?

"Let go of him!" it demanded again. This time it kicked him in the shin, too.

I winced and ducked my head, but Lord Sero only blinked. He looked down at the kid and said in an experimental sort of way, "Bad Pet!"

"He saved my life!" the kid yelled. "What did you hit him for?"

Athelas, alone of the four of them, looked amused. "We may

have acted rashly," he said. "Zero, perhaps we should put our good friend the leprechaun down to recover. He seems anxious."

"*Ajig baegopa*," said the vampire, but he put his hands in his pockets and backed away leisurely, as if that's what he'd been going to do anyway.

"We'll get you something else to eat," Athelas said to the vampire, as Lord Sero put me down on the ground very gently. "Pet will finish preparing the meal when we get home."

"I should put holy water in it," grumbled the kid.

The vampire looked startled. "*Ya! Petteu—noh—*"

"Holy water won't kill him," Lord Sero pointed out.

"No, but it makes him sneeze something flamin' good," said the kid vindictively.

"'S'cuse me," I said. "But if you've decided not to kill me, maybe I could just slip away sort of quietly—"

"What about your card?" the kid asked. "You can't get back Behind, can you?"

"I'll sort something out," I said hastily. "No need to worry yourself about me."

Athelas looked mildly amused. "What's this about his card?"

"He had one," the kid said. "Someone made it black, though. I think they did it because he wouldn't kill me."

The vampire's eyes went dark again, and he took a step forward. Lord Sero didn't move, but his voice was still cold when he asked, "So you *were* sent to kill Pet?"

"You've scared him again!" the kid said accusatorily. "Look, his wooden leg is drilling holes in the ground!"

I squeezed my eyes shut briefly and begged the kid, "*Please* stop trying to help me!" Every time it tried to help me, things got a little bit worse.

"Someone's sending people through Between," the kid said. It didn't listen real well, for someone with two ears still intact. "Far as I can tell, anyway. It's what they did to Five-Four-one. They're using normal Behindkind to murder humans, we think. They kick them through without warning, tell them to kill someone, and if they don't their cards are blackened so they can never get back. But *he* didn't kill me. I think that's what the dropbears were for, to make sure."

"Who sent you?" Lord Sero asked. If I wasn't already feeling icy to my toes, I would have frozen.

"Can't know for certain, your lordship," I said stiffly, professional instinct taking over from personal. I must be crazy.

"*Ya*," said the vampire silkily. "*Chugolae?*"

Even the kid looked worried. "He wants to kill you. Are you sure you really don't know?"

I cleared my throat. "Might have been a few odd quirks in the money trail of a company I've been following the last few months."

"What quirks?"

"Um." I glanced between Lord Sero and the vampire, unsure of which one I wanted to keep an eye on the most. "They're a group called Allied Traders; they trade with a few companies on this side of Between."

The kid blinked. "There are other humans who know about the Between and Behind?"

"You're not the only one, sunshine," I said, forgetting myself. I turned back to Lord Sero. "I mean, well, your lordship, um—well, they've been trading in what they call organic resources, but their holding sites are a front."

"No stock at any of them?"

"Not a sausage. I only caught onto them because they've been trying to be a bit clever with their taxes. Last night I told my super-visor about the investigation so I could take it up the chain."

"And this morning you find yourself thrown into the human world with orders to kill a certain human or risk never coming home," said Athelas. He was smiling. "A swift, decisive action."

"Got it in one," I said. My tone might have been a bit sour; I wasn't smiling about it all, but there was no way I was going to try and stop *him* from smiling. "And those empty warehouses—"

"Ohhh!" said the kid. It was angry again. "They've been—the *people* are the stock? I know you said they were *selling* them, but—!"

"Interesting." That was Athelas again. Trust him to find it interesting. "A two-pronged business; Behind, a human stock mill—"

"In the human world, a murder for hire set up," I nodded. "It's probably how they're paying for their human stock. Want to bet they're using all normal Behindkind for it? If I'm righteous, I can't go home to tell about it; if I'm a killer, I'm home but in as deep as they are."

"*Munjae dukae issoh*," said the vampire silkily.

"Why *two* problems?" asked the kid. "We only need to find out who's been sending Behindkind through to kill humans and stop them stealing other humans, don't we? They're the same problem."

"No, there are two problems," agreed Lord Sero.

"Perhaps three," murmured Athelas, and for what felt like the first time in ages, I grinned a bit.

Lord Sero shot him a frosty look.

"A visit to the human front of Allied Traders is in order, I think," said Athelas, ignoring both the frosty look from Lord Sero and a frowning one from the kid, who didn't understand the interaction but definitely saw it.

I grinned a bit more, because I wondered which one of them was going to tell their pet that the second problem was finding out who had hired someone to kill their pet through the intermediary of Allied Traders; or that the third problem was how that person knew this pet was cared for enough to merit being killed.

"You," Lord Sero said to me. "You're coming, too."

That wiped the grin from my face. It's probably part of why he said it. "Your lordship, they'll kill me if I go there!"

"They'll kill you if they catch you here, too," Athelas said mildly.

"Thanks," I said. "Got that idea myself."

. . .

THERE'S a certain kind of calm to company buildings Behind. Some of that is because they're rooted in the surrounding greenery to keep their assorted Fae and Other employees as happy and productive as possible. Part of it is because Fae and Other are tricky folks who love to find tricky ways around business.

There was a kind of calm to the human offices of Allied Traders, too; but this calm felt like more of a smug calm. It got up my nose because it suggested that no one could mess with them, and that anyone who did try to mess with them was going to have a bad time.

It was a good feeling to break up a bit of that calm the moment I entered the building. It was a smallish two story building in the streets of a nearby town that Lord Sero called Huonville and the kid called Hoonville, with a sarcastic twist of its mouth; old and brightly-painted on the outside, it was all fake white modernity on the inside, and I could feel the edge of Between that hung around it the minute I got in. They weren't expecting a leprechaun, and they weren't too happy to have one in there, either; all three of the secretaries in the lower level trotted after me, bleating, as I took the elevator up to the top floor.

One of them must have managed to warn the top floor, because when the doors dinged open, there was a meeting party. Well, a guy in a suit, anyway. There were a few sleek cubicles up here, with a few sleek humans pretending to work while they stole glances at me, but when they saw that I was a leprechaun, half of them rose to their feet to gawk shamelessly.

"Good evening, sirs and madams," I announced. "Please remain in your seats. Your company is being audited."

"On whose authority?" demanded the one in front of me. "Stay where you are, everyone. I'll handle this. Now, I don't know who you are, but—"

"You're the boss, are you?"

"I am the head of the board," said the human, drawing itself up. "Who are you, and what authority do you represent?"

"I'm with the BTA," I offered.

It smirked at me, which I found annoying. "Then you'd better sit down while I call your boss," it said. "I think you'll find your authority doesn't go for much around here."

"Then I suppose it's a good thing I'm not here under the authority of the BTA, isn't it?" That wiped the smug look from its face momentarily, which pleased me so much that I tapped my peg against the floor twice, smartly.

"But you said—"

"Didn't say I was here under the authority of the BTA, did I?" I reminded him.

"Then whose authority *are* you—"

"His," I said, as the elevator dinged again. I jerked my thumb behind me and cleared the way for Lord Sero, who filled the elevator doorway behind me. The human swallowed and fell back; and as it did so Lord Sero stepped through the door, Athelas and the vampire flanking him. The human kid trotted in behind them, observing the scene with interest.

"Are you the head of the board?" Lord Sero's voice could have shaken the foundations of the building—or maybe it was just me that felt the trembling right to my bones.

"Yes." That was a definite tremor in his voice. I had the feeling he knew exactly who and what Lord Sero was. "Why do you want to know?"

"I want to know who you're working with Behind, who authorised a human mill start up, and who gave you the job of killing our pet."

"Your—your *pet?*"

The kid touched one finger to its eyebrow in a salute. "Hi."

"I'm not authorised to give you that information."

The vampire Jin Yeong laughed and said something softly.

"He says," said the kid, "that it'll be more fun finding out this way, anyway."

"Pet," said Athelas, "Show the head of the board into his office for us."

The kid shrugged and went and opened the door. The head of the board walked past it, his face almost as white as Lord Sero's, and vanished within. The kid came back to stand next to me and hissed, "Won't he just call the Behind offices if we leave him alone in there?"

Athelas smiled faintly.

I said in an undertone, "That's what they're counting on."

"Doesn't make sense to me," the kid said. "Oi. I think that one's trying to sneak away."

That one was wearing a skirt, so I suppose it was female. She looked like she was trying to back away quietly, but when she bumped into Jin Yeong, who somehow managed to be behind her without a moment's notice, she sat down again very quickly.

One of the trousered ones in another cubicle asked, "Can we go? You've got our boss."

"You," said Lord Sero, "will stay. You will all stay."

"What did we do?" blustered the human. "We're employees! We're not responsible for what our company does!"

"Employees?" I laughed. I hadn't spent the last three weeks going over every inch of Allied Traders for nothing. "You're board members, every one of you!"

The female tilted her chin. "All right, what if we are? What we're doing isn't illegal, and we're making an unprecedented link between Human and Other kind."

"You tried to have me killed!" said the kid indignantly. "That's illegal over here!"

"We're not a human company," said the female. "We're a Behind company and we fall under Behind laws."

"And it's not like we've done anything but facilitate a thriving industry across borders," said another of the board members. "There's nothing you can do to us, legally!"

"Nothing according to human law," said Lord Sero, with a white, glittering smile that held no humour. "But we don't run by human law, either."

"We've done nothing against Behind law, either!"

"Between you and the dropbears," I said to the whites of all those self-righteous, terrified eyes, "I'd pick the dropbears every time. At least they only wanted to eat us; they wouldn't have tried to tell us to be grateful to help the ecosystem along."

"There's the little matter of coerced murder for hire and tampering with Identify Cards," Athelas said.

"You can't prove that!" said another of the suited ones.

The vampire laughed again.

"What an odd notion of our job you seem to have," said Athelas. "We, on the other hand, have a really very good idea of yours."

"Yeah," said the kid, scowling. "And we don't like it."

"You should go downstairs now, Pet," Athelas said pleasantly.

"What? They tried to kill me! I don't want to go!"

"Take her out," said Lord Sero to me.

Her? It was a she?

"It," said Athelas, in a reminding sort of way.

The kid said, "Oi!" at him.

"Yes, *it*!" Lord Sero snapped. "Take it out!"

I took the kid out. It protested the whole way down in the elevator, but since I was pretty sure I knew what was about to happen upstairs, I ignored the protests and dragged it out anyway. I knew that red look in Lord Sero's eyes; I'd seen it often enough in the war. Those board members, protesting and self-righteous and convinced of their own innocence, were staring death in the face.

The kid stopped complaining once we were downstairs—maybe it had expected to be kicked out at some stage. It boosted itself up on the secretary's desk and crossed its legs beneath it. "They always kick me out," it said glumly. "I mean, maybe I didn't want to be there, but if I'm part of the team I should have some of the responsibility, too."

"You're not part of the team," I said harshly. There was no way this kid should be present for what was going on upstairs. "You're the pet."

"I know they're going to kill the board members," the kid said, surprising me.

I wasn't sure if I was more surprised to know that the kid had seen through my harshness, or because it did actually know what was about to happen.

"Zero and them," it explained. "Athelas explained it to me once; their job is to investigate, judge, and apply the judgement."

"Doesn't bother you?"

"Yes," said the kid. "No. I don't know. But those board members —they're like animals. No, they're much worse than that. They think everyone else is an animal, and that they can do what they like with them. Over this side of Between, there's no other justice but Zero for humans when it comes to Behindkind problems. Human prisons can't hold Behindkind, and there are too many people Behind who turn a blind eye to that sort of thing to even try cases there. So when they start incorporating that sort of attitude and turning it into a business—"

"If it needs to be stamped out, there needs to be someone *to* stamp it out." I was a lot more certain than the kid; Lord Sero's unit might be irregular, but it was well within Behind laws. I had no problem with the way they were fixing the problem. "They're beasts, too; but they're beasts of another kind."

The kid frowned. "The *good* kind."

I thought about that for a minute. In the boardroom upstairs, three bloody emblems of death were tearing through human flesh to destroy every trace of evil from this part of the human world. And if I wasn't very much mistaken, they would soon go Behind to perform the same office there. Bloody beasts, but very necessary ones in the world of Behind.

"Yes," I said. "Beasts of a good kind."

NORTH BY TUATU

(This story takes place somewhere in the general vicinity of books six and seven. If you can get North to sit still for long enough to pinpoint exactly where, you're doing well)

DETECTIVE TUATU MISSED THE DAYS WHEN A PHONE CALL WOULD drag him from his sleep to attend a murder. The days when the only irritating sight he had to put up with at a crime scene was the stubbly, pre-coffee scowl of the forensics assistant.

These days, it seemed, the norm was for the personification of the North Wind to sweep in under his door, take her human form and crouch beside his bed to blow gently in his ear until he woke up.

It wasn't as though Detective Tuatu wasn't already busy enough. He had enough work to be going on with in his own department—not to mention the work he kept getting from a certain small human teenager who was living in one of the most dangerous situations that Tuatu had ever seen—and he wasn't really interested in forging any more relationships of the Odd and Dangerous variety.

He had a feeling that he hadn't quite seen the last of the one he was still entangled with.

He groaned and sat up, causing the bed to creak. "What do you want?"

"I need a policeman."

"Call triple-zero."

"It's not an emergency," she said. "I just need a policeman."

"Then can you *please* stop breaking into my house?"

"There was no breaking in," North told him promptly, seating herself on his bed. "I swept in through the floorboards, just like the spiders. Now if you'd told me your name—"

"I'm not telling you my name," Detective Tuatu told her grumpily. His grandmother had known better than to give first names to peoples Odd and Dangerous, and she had seen that he knew better, too. That knowledge had never before seemed necessary or relevant until this latest epoch of his life. Now it had a chill to it. "Can't you just use the phone like everyone else?"

"No," said North simply. "It's far quicker to do it this way. Besides, you've been ignoring your calls."

"How do you know that?" demanded the detective, waking up a bit more quickly. He *hadn't* been answering all of his calls, but that was because he knew how much of a headache they were going to be, and that didn't even include answering the phone to North.

"I tapped your phone," she explained. "So I knew you wouldn't answer if I did try to call you."

"That's the point of not answering calls!" Tuatu said in exasperation. "So that I have the *choice* of whether or not I talk to you! And what do you mean, you tapped my phone?"

"At any rate," said North, "if you'd told me your name, it would be much easier. I could just whisper you here on a breeze."

"That sounds like exactly the type of thing my grandmother was trying to prevent when she told me not to tell odd and dangerous people my name."

North leaned forward and much too far into Tuatu's personal

space, causing a slight blip of his heart that annoyed him greatly. "I am *very* interested in your grandmother," she said. "Can I meet her?"

"Why are you tapping my phone, North!"

"Because I want to know who's calling you, of course! You have such an interesting spectrum of acquaintance!"

"It's getting more and more interesting by the day," he said, rather sourly. He got up so that he wouldn't have to find himself sitting quite so close to her, and added, "I need to get changed."

"All right."

"That means I want you to leave the room."

"Oh." North sounded disappointed, but she did as she was told, and he found her dancing with sunbeams in the kitchen when he was dressed.

"You humans take *so long* to get dressed!" she marvelled.

"I suppose you get dressed in three seconds flat—"

"Less," she said. "But that's because the rules of the physical world don't apply to me all the time. Just when I'm being very human. I used to take a long time to get dressed, too. But that was some time ago."

She had stopped dancing, and Tuatu found that he regretted the sorrow clinging to every line of her—in her face, in the gentle droop of her shoulders, in her distant eyes. He knew something of North's momentary life as a real human, and he hadn't meant to bring up old wounds.

"What is it you need a policeman for?" he asked.

The bright smile was back on her face in a moment, and he saw her tiny feet move once, twice, lightly across the floor. She was dancing again: Tuatu had noticed that she seemed to be very fond of the first and last sunlights of the day.

"Some friends of mine asked me to help them out," she said.

"Are you sure it's something I'll be able to help with?" he asked doubtfully. "Are you sure you shouldn't be asking *those three* about it?"

"The Troika? No, I wouldn't like to bother them for something so small as this," she said. "I could do it myself, but I tend to break humans if I'm not very careful, and—"

"You have a problem with humans?" he said, filing away for later that rather disturbingly casual piece of information.

"Yes. Well, as I said before, it's not exactly my problem: it's a problem for a friend of mine. She needs a wheelchair to get around, you see, but for the last few months there has been someone parking in the only wheelchair accessible park by the doctor's office. The rest of the carpark is on a steep incline, so she can't wheel herself up as far as the front door, and her mother can't push her all the way there, either."

"I can't stop people parking in a wheelchair park if they need the park and they have a permit," Tuatu warned her. "The parks are for everyone, not just friends and family of law enforcement."

"These ones don't need it, and they don't have a permit," North said, her usually pleasant black eyes narrowing. "They don't display a permit and when I looked them up in the system—"

"North, it's *illegal* to—"

"Yes, yes," she said impatiently. "But this is *important*. When my friend asked the doctor's office about them, they pretended not to know what she was talking about. The drivers of the van don't go into the office, but my friend said you can't miss seeing their van from the office, even though they go into the aquatic centre that's under construction next door instead of the doctor's office. I could fix it myself, but—"

"I'd rather you didn't break any humans," Tuatu said hastily. "All right, all right, I'll come. I'll give them a bit of a warning and if they keep doing it, I'll issue a few fines as well. Is she *certain* they don't need the spot, permit or otherwise?"

"She tells me that they sometimes don't bother to use the wheelchair at all; they only use it if they can see people in the parking lot."

"All right," he said again. No permit was one thing; no permit and a demonstrated lack of need for the park was another. "I'm not going to arrest anyone, though."

"This is enough," said North, and she seemed pleased.

THEY TOOK Detective Tuatu's car to the doctor's office because he steadfastly refused to be carried anywhere by the North Wind. North pouted a little but got in the car anyway, and she didn't complain on the way, either. When they pulled up outside the doctor's office just outside Glenorchy, she only pointed to one of the parks—the exact one Tuatu would have used if he had been left to himself. It gave them a good view not only of the doctor's office and the carpark, but of the perennially closed aquatic centre next door. It made him wonder exactly how often North had been on stakeout, and for what purposes.

"There's nothing there," Tuatu said, indicating the empty parking spot.

"The surgery isn't open yet," North replied. "Just wait. There's five minutes to go; they should arrive any minute."

As she was still speaking, Tuatu saw a white van in the rear-view mirror, slowing and with its indicator blinking.

"Right on time," he said. "It looks like one of the doctors has arrived, too."

The doctor was a messy, plump, pleasant-looking woman who shot a very narrow-eyed, school-marmish look at the car they were in. That made Tuatu feel slightly better, because if she had noticed that it was odd for a car to be simply sitting in the carpark in this area, then it was likely that she knew all about the van, and that it was something the surgery had allowed.

That was what he thought, right up until the driver of the van got out, walked calmly to the back of the van, took out his wheelchair, and stood beside it. Tuatu would have gotten out then, but the wheelchair ramp came down after the man, and a teenaged boy in a bright red wheelchair rolled out onto the bitumen.

The doctor's gaze didn't even falter as she walked across the lot; it swept past the van, past the man who was now taking a short run up before free-wheeling down the hill toward the aquatic centre, his wheelchair backwards, past the young boy who coasted down the hill after the older man.

"The heck!" Tuatu said in astonishment. "Did she not see them? What did *I* just see? Is it just the kid who needs a chair?"

If so, why was the adult male using one? And why was he using it like a showground ride?

"Oh," said North. Her voice was thoughtful. "Well, this changes things a little."

"What does?" he asked, still watching the two males as they took the wheelchair ramp at the aquatic centre at a very fast clip.

"Follow me," she said, and got out of the car.

"Wait!" Tuatu protested, fumbling at the door handle; too slow to do anything but dash after her. "There's no need for you to get involved! I'll have a word with them myself! At least one of them seems to need the chair."

North said decisively, "I don't think so. They may not be dangerous on their own, but there's sure to be more of them."

"More of who? Park stealers?"

"And they're always more dangerous when there's more of them," she called over her shoulder.

Her feet moved too quickly for him to be able to distinguish them; Tuatu was quite sure she wasn't exactly human right now.

"If they're more dangerous, we should make a plan before we go in!" he called ahead to her, but she didn't slow down.

"I don't plan things," she said. "We sweep in, and we sweep out, and we sweep everything before us."

"All right, but there's no point in speaking in the royal we when it's just you and me," he retorted, catching up with her finally at the door. "Do you *have* to run so fast?"

"Yes," she said, her eyes sparkling. "You wouldn't let me bring you here, so I needed to feel a little bit of speed."

"You could have wound down the window," said Tuatu, before he could stop himself. He had been half expecting her to do as much.

North grinned at him, but became serious almost the next minute, as changeable as her name. "You should stay behind me," she said. "Just in case."

"Just in case *what*?" he demanded, looking around the aquatic centre's carpark that had been filled with construction supplies, and into the empty centre itself. "It was two men!"

"Where there's two, there's always more," North said solemnly, and darted in through the door.

The centre smelled...*odd* when Detective Tuatu followed her into the centre, trying to stop himself protesting that she should be staying behind him when he knew how ridiculous that was. It wasn't a musty smell or a chlorine smell; nor was it the smell of dust. It was something distinctly fishier than that. Fishy, and perhaps a little bit slimy—the detective felt that he could find himself stepping on something unpleasantly squishy any moment.

"Where do you think they went?" he asked North quietly, as they moved through the chilly entrance area. "I wouldn't have thought they were likely to be doing anything related to drugs, but this place looks like it's been closed for the last year, and if the door was already open for them—"

"It's not drugs," said North. "And they'll be at the pool."

Tuatu would have liked to have asked her how she knew as much, but as soon as they entered the main pool area, he could see that she was quite right: of the older male there was no sign, but the teenaged male still sat in his chair with his back to them, facing the deep end of the pool.

"Aha!" said North triumphantly. "Come here, you slimy little crustacean!"

She seized the teenager by the back of the collar and hefted him out of the chair without so much as a grunt of effort, then threw him directly into the pool.

"North!" Tuatu expostulated, appalled. "You can't throw people into pools! Especially not when they can't walk!"

He started forward as he spoke, ready to dive in and save the struggling teen, but North's tiny hand closed on his elbow with stunning power.

"They're not people," she said. "Watch."

Under Detective Tuatu's disbelieving eyes, the pair of legs thrashing beneath the water rippled, joined, and became…a tail. The newly outed merman surfaced, cursing, and called North a few choice names that sparked in Tuatu a new desire to jump into the water, though for very different reasons this time.

"They're merpeople," North added. "They don't usually need the wheelchairs—they just don't like having to walk when they're in the world above."

"You can't out me to humans!" the teenager yelled at her.

"You can't take over swimming pools and carparks!" North retorted. "Where's your school leader?"

"None of your business, ground crawler!"

Tuatu opened his mouth to warn the teenager that he was already facing charges of trespass and breaking and entering, but as he did so, there was a crowding of shadows at the doors behind them. Five men, he noticed, with the clear, cool realisation that if North wasn't as powerful as he suspected she was, they were in a great deal of trouble.

"I'm right here," said the barrel-chested man at the front of the group. It was very easy to see that chest, not only because of its size but because it was bare and very, very white. "Who's asking?"

"Police," Tuatu said shortly, showing his identification. "Who are you, and what are you doing here?"

"This is our place now, ground crawler," said the leader, and pulled a gun from the back of his waistband. "If the owner has sent you to make trouble for us, well, you're going to run into a bit of trouble yourself."

Tuatu was fairly certain it was only a tranquiliser gun, but he reached back and grabbed North's hand to tug her behind him anyway, his identification still presented rather mulishly in front of him with the ridiculous thought that it could somehow help.

North, unfortunately, did not budge an inch. "Don't be ridiculous," she said to the barrel-chested leader. "I assume you know very well who I am."

"I do," said the leader, and pulled the trigger.

North gave a very small, surprised gasp, and staggered back a pace, dropping Tuatu's hand. A dart, protruding from her shoulder, wobbled as she dropped to one knee, and the detective wasn't sure whether he or North appeared more surprised in the reflective glass walls around the pool.

"North?" he said sharply. He hadn't expected something so small as a tranquiliser dart to put down the North Wind. "Do you need a hand?"

"No," she said, too quickly. "It would be better if you don't touch me, I think."

"That's the problem with you incarnations," said the leader, to Tuatu's further bemusement. "You're always getting too close to the human world."

"What's he talking about?"

"Nothing to worry about," North said, her voice cheerful but faint. "Just don't touch me and I'll be fine. Probably don't talk to me for a few minutes, either; I'd rather you didn't concern yourself with me at the moment."

That cut at Detective Tuatu's heart, because he didn't see why North should be allowed to sweep into his house, blow in his ear, dance with sunbeams in his kitchen, and then tell him not to be concerned with her.

He drew his gun.

"Don't point that stupid human thing at us," the merman leader said. "It won't stop us; it'll only annoy us."

"I enjoy being annoying," said Tuatu, sparing a quick glance behind him at North. She had pulled out the dart and was again standing, but she didn't look quite steady. If his only weapon was a mere annoyance to these people, he would need to find a different weapon: he couldn't count on North to look after them both when she was still swaying on her feet.

He looked around them as far as he could without being obvious about it, but all he could see was the button that unfurled the plastic pool covers, and that was no use unless—unless he could unfurl it very quickly in a particular direction...

"You won't enjoy it by the time we're finished with you," said the merman. "We'll see how you like a bit of fun with the boys. You can't threaten us."

Detective Tuatu met North's eyes in the glassy reflection of the wall, and flicked his eyes back to the switch. He saw her look at the furled pool cover and grin.

"I haven't threatened you," he said to the men. "Not yet, anyway. I'm about to begin."

"Do what you want," jeered one of the mermen behind the leader. "You can't take our pool from us."

All he needed, thought Tuatu, was for them to move forward a *little* bit more. In line with that pool cover roll across the water, for example, so that it could easily envelop them were there to be a strong enough breeze.

"It's time for you to get in the water," said the merman leader. "If you do us a favour and jump in without us having to put you in, we'll even let you up to breathe now and then."

"Come and get us," said Tuatu, banking on the merman's overweening machismo. He added, for good measure, "Fish breath."

It was a safe bet: the merman surged forward with a snarl of annoyance, forgetting his dart gun, and the other four followed him. Tuatu let them get uncomfortably close before he pressed the button, and for a very horrible moment, he thought he'd left it too long.

Then there was a roar of wind, and the scream of plastic whipping through the air at high speed. A brief tornado of wind and plastic tore around the group of five mermen while the teenager yelled threats and insults from the pool and struggled to climb out again, then there was only a very vocal bundle of plastic struggling on the cold pool tiles and one rapidly calming teenager who had just realised the precarity of his situation.

"Nice work," said Tuatu, to North.

She smiled brightly at him. "See how well we work together! Aren't you glad you came with me? It was much more interesting than I thought it would be: such fun!"

"Oi," said a familiar voice from across the pool, while Tuatu was trying to find a way to express how very much he disagreed with her point of view. "Couldn't you lot wait five seconds for us? We were coming."

The teenaged merman disappeared in the flip of a tail, and Tuatu saw him beneath the water, trying to cower behind the pool cleaner. That wasn't surprising: across the pool was a trio of Behind-kind and one scrawny human. The scrawny human was Pet, Detective Tuatu's friend and current thorn-in-the-side: she wasn't exactly deadly, though he had the feeling that if she stayed with the people she was staying with for much longer, she might very well be.

What had frightened the merman, however, was the massive, pale fae lord at the front of the group—Lord Sero, apparently, though Detective Tuatu knew him as Zero. If Zero's imposing presence and hard, cold blue eyes weren't enough to frighten anyone, the fae lord was flanked by Athelas on his left; a brown-eyed, gently smiling, quietly terrifying fae steward who knew far too much about everything in general and death in particular to leave Detective Tuatu comfortable. On Zero's right was a gorgeously suited, perfectly pressed, almost glowingly handsome Korean man— vampire, as Tuatu was quite well aware. The vampire's pout and liquid dark eyes seemed to suggest that he had come for blood and had not as yet been satisfied. Tuatu, who had seen exactly what it took to satisfy the vampire, understood perfectly why the teenaged merman didn't break the surface.

All four of them skirted the pool and approached: Pet grinning, Zero slightly frowning.

Of North, who was bubbling over with laughter, Tuatu asked resignedly, "Was this all a joke? A Between surprise party or something?"

"No," said North, still giggling. "But my friend *did* say that there were a lot of suspicious looking people around yesterday and now I understand why!"

"Rude!" said Pet, but she was still grinning. "Suspicious, me? I've got a very trustworthy face!"

"They were probably talking about the fae lord with a knife belt and the vampire with blood all down his face," Tuatu said.

"I should like to point out that he does not at present have blood on his face," Athelas gently mentioned. Despite the gentleness of his voice, the mere sound of it caused the bundle of mermen to become deathly silent and cease their struggles. "Moreover, what sinister appearance do I present?"

"I don't know," Tuatu said. "But I know you're not harmless."

"I should think not!" said Athelas, even more gently, and turned to assist Zero, who had silently begun to unpackage the sardined mermen.

"I am trying to be very good," said the vampire, leaning an elbow on Pet's shoulder. "But I would like to *bite* someone."

The cold smile that accompanied the information, along with the fact that JinYeong had said something understandable at all, instead of in Korean, suggested to Tuatu that he was the person JinYeong would like to bite.

Tuatu cleared his throat and looked away. He asked Pet, "Did he just speak English?"

"Nah," said Pet. "He must've decided to let you understand him for once."

"To let—Is he getting in my head to do that?"

"Nah, he's just using a—um, translator."

Tuatu narrowed his eyes at her. "I don't believe you. Why does he still want to bite someone, by the way? He's usually been pretty busy biting people by the time he gets to me."

"Yeah, well, that's the problem: he *hasn't* been. This lot only go troppo on Behindkind when they're causing harm to humans. Merfolk having a bar mitzvah every few days and stealing disabled carparks isn't causing harm to humans, just being a pain in the neck."

"*I* would like," said JinYeong, more quietly this time but no less stubbornly, "to be a pain in the neck."

"I think I preferred it when I couldn't understand the vampire," Tuatu said. "Is that—is that what was happening? The merfolk were taking over the centre to host *parties*? They pulled a gun on North!"

"It was only a tranquiliser gun," North said dismissively. "They probably thought it wasn't going to work on me: they were just playing."

"Yes," said the vampire, tilting his head to look at North, and then at Tuatu. "It is *verrrry* interesting. But if they had played with you, it would have been unpleasant."

"Yeah, we saved a bloke from one of 'em the other night," Pet explained. "They nearly drowned him, but he got out onto the road. Figured he'd come from in here and thought we'd see what was going on next time someone arrived."

"What's Zero saying to them?" asked Detective Tuatu, looking curiously across at the five cowering mermen and the one teenager who had been as unceremoniously dragged from the water by Zero as he had been thrown in by North. Zero towered over them, even the barrel-chested one, and he wasn't surprised at their change of attitude. "Why can't I understand it?"

"He's telling 'em that if they don't watch their p's and q's, he's gunna let you arrest the lot of 'em and they can see how dry their precious scales get when they're rotting in jail," said Pet, grinning. "And you can't understand 'em because he's doing the reverse of what JinYeong's doing."

Tuatu very nearly grinned. No wonder the merfolk had been

gazing over at him with expressions of horrified disbelief for the last few minutes.

"Is he going to stop them coming here?"

"Nope," said Pet. "They're allowed to use the pool; they're citizens as well. But they have to hire it out the same as everyone else, and they've got to clear away all the stuff that makes it look like the centre's under renovation. *And* they have to pay the fee to have the pool cleaned every time they use it for one of their parties, to get rid of the gunk."

"Tell them they have to stop using the disabled park next door, as well," the detective said, stepping forward to address Zero. "If they do that again, I'll lock 'em up and throw away the key."

Zero's pale brows rose: Tuatu couldn't tell if the fae was irritated or impressed, but since it didn't seem likely that he would be impressed by Tuatu, the detective came to the conclusion that Zero was irritated.

Still, Zero asked the mermen, "Did you hear that?"

The mermen nodded quickly and silently, without looking up, and Zero raised his brows once again in Detective Tuatu's direction.

"Are you satisfied, Detective?"

"Yes," said Detective Tuatu, retreating to the relative safety of North, Pet, and the vampire. North gave him an approving pat on the shoulder, which made Tuatu feel far more exhilarated than he would have expected, and Pet grinned at him once again.

"If we're done here, we might as well go back home for a barbie," she said.

Detective Tuatu hadn't quite been holding his breath, but he must have been tensing, because he discovered that his jaw was tight only when he relaxed. He knew something of the methods of these three non-humans, and their methods usually involved a more...permanent solution to misbehaviour.

"Told ya," said Pet, who had been watching him narrowly. "A telling off is all they're getting."

"No one need die today," Zero said, but he said it toward the mermen, and Tuatu was left with the feeling that it was a warning, not a comfort. "You can go."

The mermen shuffled out, dragging the soggy teenager with them and murmuring various iterations of, "Thank you m'lord", "Yes, m'lord", and "As you say, m'lord".

Zero watched them until they were gone, his broad back turned to the rest of the group, relentless in his watchfulness.

"You came close to minor disaster today, my lady," murmured Athelas to North. "It can be such a...humanising sensation, interacting with the denizens of this world."

"Nonsense," North said, putting her nose up a little. "As if a few mermen would be a problem!"

"That," said Zero, turning to pierce her with a cool blue look, "was not what Athelas was referring to. I've already warned you about this sort of thing: if you want to be safe, you shouldn't get attached to humans."

"That's only good if you want to stay alive," said North, with barely-concealed exuberance. "I want to *live*."

Detective Tuatu opened his mouth to ask exactly what they were talking about, but Pet got in first.

"C'mon, you lot," she said. "I've got steak out on the bench and if it goes bad, *I'm* not going to the supermarket to get more."

"I love steak," said North, grabbing Detective Tuatu's hand. "And I love not cooking even more! If you ask me very nicely, I'll carry you there so quickly—"

"I'm not telling you my name," the detective said.

"But—"

"No."

"Later, then," she said irrepressibly. "I'll come and visit you tomorrow morning to see if you've changed your mind."

"I don't—" began Tuatu, but it was too late; he was talking to the wind. North now sat demurely in his car, as if she'd been there all along.

"Catch ya at the house," said Pet, winking; then she, and the vampire, and the two fae were gone.

Tuatu found himself content to take the human way around. After all, even if the incarnation of the North Wind was waiting in his car, for a little while she had been human enough to take a dart to the shoulder.

And that was something Tuatu felt should be encouraged.

ALL THE DIFFERENT SHADES OF BLUE

(After six but before seven, this is my closed-room scenario in homage to one of my favourite tv shows: Leverage)

THERE'S A SHARPNESS TO THE HUMAN WORLD. AN EDGE TO THE wind that bites, a piercing sensation to the jagged pieces of sound that litter the perilously light air, a poniard point to the sound of human voices duelling inside the confinement of a café or a restaurant.

It's not like that beneath the waves. Beneath the waves there's softness and peace and all the different shades of blue you ever saw or heard or smelled. A comfortable feeling of weight pressing against every part of you that keeps you exactly where you're meant to be. Beneath the waves—ah, if I could, that's where I'd live out all my days.

If I could—and there's the rub.

There's not much of a life Beneath for a half-breed merman; particularly not for one born without gills, or the lung strength necessary to stay below the waves for more than a couple of minutes at a time. I can thank my human mother for that—just like I can thank my merman father for the disjointed and utterly useless bones in my lower half. Neither human nor mer, those bones don't join enough to be used for walking, though in my mer-form they make a serviceable tail. Enough to get by, if I could but breathe beneath the waves. Above the waves, I can breathe, and perhaps that would be enough to get by, too—if only I could walk.

To the rest of the Other Kind, there's Behind, Between, and the human world. To us merfolk, there's Above and Beneath—the airy side, and the real world. The only laws that really matter to us are the laws Beneath, even when we're above. Perhaps that's why I became a hacker when my parents abandoned me in the Above world; it was a combination of orphan angst and an ingrained disregard for human laws.

Besides all that, my job means I don't have to go out if I don't wish to do so. It's not a simple matter to navigate my wheelchair around the bends in the outdated and rusty ramp that runs around the outside of my building. Perhaps I could move to another flat, but there aren't many places around North Hobart where you can have a beautiful view *and* space for a water tank the size I need—not within my budget, at any rate.

So I put up with the difficulty and go out every day for my coffee. Coffee and a smile, that's the way I think of it.

It was a Thursday that day. Busy, as usual, and I had to be careful crossing the road because there are no zebra crossings there. The traffic is inclined to be savage and suicidal in North Hobart, and although there are small ramps for wheelchair access to the road, there's a good chance the drivers won't see you above the guard rails. If they do, there's more than a chance they'll attempt to drive over you regardless.

In spite of that, I made it safely to the other side, the momentum from my dash carrying me up the small ramp and halfway across the footpath. I was earlier than usual, as I had been for the past week at least. I usually take my coffee-and-a-smile at eleven o'clock, but when I accept a job, I like to start as early in the day as possible. I should have known better than to take a job across the road from my house, but the money was more than usually good, and it wasn't a difficult job.

Potentially illegal and most definitely Other, but not difficult. Perhaps you could call it delicate.

The café sat above a Behind club that didn't quite exist in the human world—normal, warm, and reasonably popular. It had human owners, naturally, but whether or not they knew it, they paid a tax to the Behindkind beneath them. Lately they hadn't been drawing as many customers as the Behindkind thought convenient for a cover, and I had been hired to alter the ancient protective spells around the cafe to allow something a little...extra...in the magics.

If it was only a matter of hacking the magic it would still have been illegal, at least by Behind laws—in law, if not in practise, Behindkind doesn't approve of meddling with humans. But by human laws it was illegal, too; to run the program I would be hacking directly into the café's internal network and accessing their music tracks. The club below and the café above might be linked Behind, but they certainly weren't linked on paper or legally.

It could also, technically, be called fraud. Even if it wasn't music, the track I would be threading through the café's music was specially designed to make its patrons more open-fisted, not to mention more inclined to return. The club below would benefit not only from a larger revenue, but from the innocent front created by a bustling coffee house.

Goblins, it would seem, didn't understand the correlation between selling good coffee and a bustling customer base. Not that I should be talking myself out of a job, but the coffee had always been good enough to bring repeat customers before the human management changed.

In any case, they gave me the ambient track, laced with magic, and it was my job to make sure it took. For a very good fee, naturally.

As a program, it needed to infect the system and all the computerised bits, of course; but my real hacking is the kind that isn't limited to computerised systems. In fact, most of the hacking I do for Behindkind clients is the kind of hacking that involves infiltrating magical systems with malicious magic or hijacking them with load-bearing magic. Routine, human hacking jobs aren't exactly rare, but when my client is Behindkind, the odds are my job will be one that involves magic.

I'd been working on this particular job for nearly a week now. And yet, it shouldn't have been a difficult job. All I should have had to do was hack into the network and then into the threaded filaments of protection that hung around the coffee shop so that it would allow me to make potentially dangerous alterations in the magic of the cafe. The protection must have been from some long gone owner or patron, because the previous owners had run the café as long as I'd been patronising it, and they were no Behindkind. It was nearly impossible to detect; thin and delicate, that enchantment should have been weak, too, but for some reason it clung to everything I tried to do, sticking like spider web to my attempts to break through it and fouling every magical hack I tried besides. It left me curious to know who had once loved this coffee shop enough to ward it against the kind of magic that needed such protections, and more than slightly irritated at the failure of every test run I'd tried so far.

I checked my watch as I worked. Nearly eleven: so that was why my magic had begun to feel sluggish. Eleven o'clock was coffee-and-a-smile time.

My fingers slowed until they were no longer typing. I would have to check the last few lines of script I'd input; there were bound to be mistakes, and though my typing wasn't producing actual lines of code, it was producing something far more volatile—lines of magic. Far less dangerous to make mistakes with my computerised code than with my magic code.

I sat back against the soft fabric curve of my wheelchair as the hour hand of my watch ticked over to eleven. If I cupped my hands around the coffee mug like so, it would look as though I was taking a natural break, cool and unconcerned. As though I wasn't waiting for a flicker of dark blue jeans and black boots along the lower part of the window that would mean—

There was a flicker of blue, and I looked away immediately. I didn't like to be seen looking when she walked up to the door. It was enough that at the tinkling of the bell, I couldn't ever help looking up...

The bell on the door tinkled lightly.

I looked up, my fingers tightening around the coffee mug, and there she was at the door. Long-legged and thin, she had a kind of faun-like look about her. I wasn't sure if that was because of her thinness, or if it was the hopeful, almost wide-eyed way she seemed to look at the world around her. Her mouth was thin, too, and just a bit crooked, which is probably why I didn't seem to be able to help smiling at her when she came in for her coffee every day.

To a Behinder's eyes, she could have been called ugly—to the constantly glamorous Behindkind, every other creature is ugly, and even among Behindkind there's none so beautiful as the merpeople. Even for a human, she wasn't pretty; her nose was too big, her mouth too thin, and her long, dark hair was perpetually untidy. But I couldn't help smiling whenever I saw her face, just the same. Perhaps I've been in the human world for too long.

I smiled by reflex today, too, and she smiled back at me. I don't know who she is, but she comes for coffee nearly every day, just like me. She must have a tab set up with the human owner, because I've never seen her pay.

I probably should have tried to warn her away when the ownership changed and the profits shrank enough for those below to notice—goblins with a Behindkind clientele aren't the safest combination for a human to be around. I didn't warn her, because at heart I'm as selfish as the next Behindkind; and if I was telling the truth, I liked her smile.

Now she would continue walking, the smile still sitting lopsidedly on her face, and buy her coffee: three large, with lids. It happened the same way every time.

Except, perhaps, today.

Today, she didn't keep walking, and I saw the smile fade from her face by degrees, replaced by a thoughtful, interested kind of look. It was an odd expression for such a young face to wear.

She glanced back at the door for the briefest moment, then around at the café—a quick, flickering look all around. As I watched, she blinked and began walking again. They say a human's feet point in the direction they're most wanting to go, but her feet never shifted, despite that glance at the door. She passed by my chair as she always did, and went to the counter for her coffee. She would have three coffees to take away, just as I always had my one in a mug, and I would smile at her once again when she turned to close the glass door. That was what had happened since she had started coming to the café.

To say that I was surprised, therefore, when she slid into the booth at right angles from me a moment later, would be to greatly understate the situation.

"Hi," she said. Her hands were wrapped around a coffee mug; they were slender, capable hands, but it was her eyes that were really arresting. I hadn't seen her close enough before to know that they were such a light, luminous grey. "I'm Pet."

I was surprised at the warmth that blossomed in my chest. She didn't look shy, this girl; but she gave the impression of self-sufficiency that I would have said was at odds with the kind of personality required to make the first move on a stranger. Or *was* she making a move?

"Hi," I said back, and started to close my laptop. It wouldn't matter if I took a break. "I'm Marazul."

"No, no," she said. "No need to stop. You work here now? The last few days, you've been over here typing."

I pushed the screen open again and edged it just a little further

Between the human world and Behind, so that it looked like the simple laptop it ought to look like. I do use the laptop bit of it for human-type hacking, but it's really mostly an interface for the trickier job of magical hacking.

"I don't, in general. I'm freelancing for them this week."

"Ah." Pet nodded solemnly. "I thought you had a bit more stuff than you usually have. Where do you fit it all?"

She glanced over at my wheelchair, and I felt a touch of unease. My workbox usually stayed Between until I needed it: in the human world, it looked like a small laptop sleeve that I could slip into the seat of my wheelchair, between my outer thigh and the side of my chair. When I needed it, all I needed to do was bring it from Between into the human world. Unfortunately, I had just brought it properly into the human side to rummage for a particular piece of something that I was attempting to help along my magical efforts. There was certainly nothing on my chair that could have been used to harness a workbox of that size, nor a compartment big enough to house it.

"Someone carried it over for me," I said, with barely a pause, nodding at the building across the road that supported my apartment. "I only live across the road."

"Ah," Pet said again. The thoughtful look was back on her face, and if it had sat oddly on her face before, now it was something else again. Thoughtful, interested—and perhaps a touch wary?

I found myself, ridiculously, ashamed of myself for lying to her. Who ever heard of Behindkind being apologetic for lying to humans? It's not only good policy, it's almost tradition.

Oblivious, Pet sipped her coffee, sighing her contentment in rainbow-spangled steam. She let me work for a few minutes in silence before she asked, "Are you hurt?"

I looked instinctively at my hands. Sometimes I don't feel it when I cut myself on the Airy side. "What? Am I bleeding?"

She stared a bit, and then grinned. "Oh! Right! Sorry. I meant the wheelchair. Did you have an accident?"

"No," I said, and went back to my work. The spell hack hadn't taken in any of my earlier tests, and I didn't like that. That's the most absurd thing about working magic through electronics—sometimes it takes up without so much as a pull, and other times it refuses utterly to work. "I was born like this."

"Oh." She nodded. "I thought it might be a cover."

"A cover?" I couldn't help smiling. Her tone was just the right mix of gusto and speculation to make me think she was the kind of human girl who snuck around the town hoping for dark deeds and nefarious characters.

"Yeah!" She nodded again, this time more enthusiastically. "A few of the merpeople I know don't like to walk, so they go around in wheelchairs when they're above."

I kept smiling, but I had the distinct sensation that I couldn't breathe. "Did you say *merpeople*?"

She actually shushed me. "What if someone hears you?"

"What are—What *are* you?"

"Me? I'm just a human."

"That's what I mean," I said, frowning. My fingers hovered over the keyboard as I tried to decide where the greater part of my attention should be fixed—Pet, or my merger program. "You're just a human. What do you know about merpeople?"

"Not a lot. I can't breathe underwater, so I don't meet many."

"That's not what I really meant." I sat back in my chair, genuinely curious and just a little bit amused. "You're very good at not answering questions, for a human."

"Aren't I!" she agreed, looking pleased and pink. "I'm getting a bit of practise, these days. I suppose your mother was human."

I nodded, unobtrusively twitching something within the program right with a touch of magic and a tap at the keyboard. The merger program turned the electronic pulse into a magical one that faded seamlessly into the threads of protection around the café.

Wonderful! I would be able to run another test soon.

"She was. How did you know?"

"Athelas says that if the mother is human, problems always come out on the human side, and if the father is human, they come out on the Other side."

My fingers curled away from the keyboard completely as a warmth of amusement sprang up in me. For a human, she really was adorable. How did she know these things—and why *these* things in particular?

My test, I thought, could wait a few minutes more. I asked, "Does he? What else does he say?"

"Mostly *don't do that, Pet*, and *must you, Pet?*" she said. She leaned forward, edging her elbows onto the table, and asked, "What are you doing, anyway? Your computer is halfway Between, did you know? I'm not even sure it's a real computer."

If I had been looking down at my keyboard, my head would have snapped up. As it was, the café felt as though it shook a little. I said in some shock, "I'm aware."

It wasn't what I had meant to say, but it didn't seem to strike Pet as odd. She said, "Oh well, as long as you know. I suppose that's how you got everything here."

"It is," I agreed, aware once again that I still hadn't said what I intended to say.

"You lied to me."

Was that a current of disappointment in her voice?

"Behindkind usually *do* lie to humans," I pointed out; and this time, it was what I meant to say. I didn't like the reproach in her eyes. Because of that reproach, I added, "If you knew, why did you ask me?"

"Wanted to see if you'd lie to me," Pet said laconically. "Is it because you're trying to push a spell through the protection around the café?"

"Do you really think it's wise for a human who knows a little too much to be asking questions of strangers?" I asked her; and if it was a little sharp, well, I was still taken aback. A girl who smiled at someone so friendlily as Pet did had no business being so sharp—or so knowledgeable.

"That's another thing Athelas says," said Pet.

She really was very good at not answering questions. I would need all my attention if I was to find out exactly who and what she was. I set the latest test hack running with a few clicks of my mouse and a very small amount of magic to push it Between, where it would pull Behind and the human world a little closer than usual.

It wouldn't work, of course—not when it still had that annoyingly sticky protection spell to contend with, not to mention the mistakes in the script that I had probably made due to Pet's arrival and proximity. But it would give me some idea of what I needed to do next, and at least it would look as though I were still doing my job if the goblins thought to check on me.

I pushed the laptop slightly to the side, leaning back in my chair with an assumption of ease that I didn't quite feel, and asked her, "Who is Athelas?"

"Flaming heck!" said Pet, stiffening. "What was that?"

I couldn't help laughing. "That's not even a deflection!" I said. "You can do better than that!"

"No," she said, covering one ear with a grimace and opening and closing her mouth as if she was trying to pop that ear. "I'm not kidding. What did you do?"

"What do you mean?" She couldn't be talking about my test hack, but I looked down at the laptop screen instinctively, anyway.

Much to my surprise, it was running perfectly, load-bearing magic and protective spell in perfect harmony. I frowned at it. I'd have to go through and see exactly what I'd written into the script that had finally gotten it past the threads of protection that had stalled every previous attempt. In my business, it pays to learn as you go.

Pet stood, still covering that one ear. "Rats," she said. "I was hoping I was wrong. Hey, is your laptop connected to the internet, or is it only for Between magic?"

"What are you doing?"

She took a few steps away from the booth and tugged on the door handle. Much to my surprise, it didn't move.

Pet jerked a thumb at it. "Checking this. It's not locked."

"If it's not locked, why can't you open it?"

"Yeah, well; that's the point, isn't it?" she said, returning to the table to take up her coffee cup again. "That's why I want to know what you just did."

More defensively, I said, "I didn't do anything."

Her face was ridiculously clear to read. I saw her lips twist downward, the faintest suggestion of movement that brought a distinct tinge of sorrow to her face. Reproachfully, she said, "You're still lying to me."

"It's just a test hack," I said, before I knew what I was doing. "I didn't expect it to work."

Pet looked suspicious. "It wasn't a computer thing," she said. "It was—well, I don't actually know *what* it was, but I know it's not a computer thing."

"It's..." I paused, trying to come up with a way to explain it to a human, before I remembered that she already knew about the city Behind. "I'm a hacker. But I don't just hack computers and networks."

Her eyes narrowed over her coffee cup. "You hack *magic*? How does that work?"

"If I told everyone that, I wouldn't be able to make a living," I said.

Pet grinned. "Don't have magic," she said. "I'm human."

"Then how would you know if there's something going on or not?"

"Three things," said Pet. "One, the counter boy was new today, and he's nicked off while I've been talking to you. Two, I saw the bits of magic you've been trying—"

"What?"

"Said I didn't *have* magic," she said. "Didn't say I can't see it."

I looked at her sideways, shaken but unwilling to be completely thrown off. "Magic isn't visible to humans."

"Yeah, that's what Athelas says, but I can see it all right." She thought about that, and admitted, "Well, not exactly the magic. More like the mess it makes Between when it isn't done right. And I heard the thing that started up when you did something with your computer just now."

"*What* thing?" I demanded. I layered my voice with just a touch of magic, and, more devastatingly, a combination of amusement and slight condescension. Older brother looking at a silly younger sister with a too-big imagination. "I haven't even begun the proper program yet—just a test one."

"Yeah?" said Pet again, and she sounded annoyed. "Well, what's wrong with everyone here, then?"

"Nothing is wrong with them," I said, flicking a look around the room. "They might want to buy a few more cups of coffee, but only when I feed the real thing through the hack."

Pet took a sip of coffee and exhaled another variegated breath of steam. Her face wasn't unreadable—there were myriad emotions and thoughts passing across that glass-like surface—but there were so many thoughts, passing so swiftly, that it might as well have been unreadable. Impossible to tell what she was thinking—what she might do. At least, I found myself thinking, in rather guilty relief, the door was shut, and she couldn't get out.

She couldn't *do* anything, either. A human couldn't—a human couldn't—

And then Pet reached out.

She reached out in the human world, and reached *right through into Between*. One finger touched the top of my laptop, pushing gently, and it began to emerge from Between space into the human world.

The laptop flickered, grew; it *expanded*.

"Stop it!" I said, and shoved the laptop back Between. "It's not—"

"I know," Pet said, agreeably. "It's not really a laptop. It just looks like one in this part of reality. What is it when it's Behind? I can't see all of it; it's too big."

"You can't do things like that in public!" I said, too startled to sound anything else but angry. "Don't you know better than make trouble in front of humans?"

Pet looked questioningly at me. "What d'you mean, public?"

"There's a whole café full of—"

"Humans," Pet finished for me. "Yeah, but d'you notice anything about them?"

"What do you mean?"

I looked around at the humans. They were talking relaxedly to each other, smiling and gesturing and sipping their coffee. As if they hadn't seen my laptop grow, or change; as if they hadn't seen the space around us expand. It was lucky, I thought, that no one had been looking. The café looked perfectly normal; nothing was out of the ordinary.

Then I looked around again, a slight frown sinking between my brows. Nothing out of the ordinary, if it wasn't for the fact that they were just a little bit muffled, or slow, or maybe just less sharp than usual.

"Try to talk to one of 'em," advised Pet. "Bet they won't hear you. That one's eating the same bite of muffin every time he takes a bite, and the one over there has leant forward three times in a row while we've been talking, and done the exact same square with her fingers."

I looked around again, and this time I saw what she meant. The humans, each and every one of them, were repeating the same cycle of a minute or two, over and over again.

A feeling of annoyance, edged with fear, welled up within me. Had the goblins been up to their old tricks? A long time ago, there had been a problem with humans slipping Between and eating goblin food, thus trapping themselves Behind for as long as the goblins chose to keep them. Goblins, the avaricious peddlers of the

Behind world, had been luring humans through twilit Between markets, and selling them on to anyone who cared to have a thralled human. The scheme hadn't ended well for the humans, but it had been a true disaster for the goblins—and anyone who had traded in human lives.

In those days, there had been a rumour of a lone revenger of human wrongs, and many injustices that wouldn't have been taken up by the Behind courts had been dealt with in a quiet, savage way.

These days, there was a newer rumour. Even Behindkind like myself, living on the human side of Between, knew about the human trader offices that had been ripped apart and sunk into bloody oblivion a few months ago by a mysterious group of three known as the Troika. We all knew about it; we all knew we could be next if we allowed ourselves to be too free with the humans around us.

And I—I had just allowed myself to be used in a scheme to entrap humans, whether or not I'd known it at the time.

"This," I said, with a dry throat, "this wasn't meant to happen. It's just a test run of a new program to encourage humans to spend a bit more while they're here."

"Reckon?" Pet gazed up at me. "What about the music, then? What's that for?"

I was about to tell her that there wasn't any music—even the track they'd given me was only ambient sound—when I heard it. It must have been working away in the background for so long that I couldn't even remember when it started.

"Isn't that the café's music?"

"Nope." Pet tipped up her coffee cup to catch the last drops of liquid and put it down on the tabletop with a small, precise *tap*. She was smiling; a glad, relieved thing that told me she hadn't been sure I wasn't the one doing whatever it was that was happening around the café.

She said, "Reckon it's been going since I got here, but when you did that thing on your magic computer, it got *really* loud. Like it properly activated, or something. I reckon whatever was in your hack was half of whatever other half they were already playing. Think you can stop it?"

Stop it? I could barely hear it. Every time I thought I had an idea of what the melody was, it slipped away—or maybe just slipped through my consciousness—and I forgot what I was listening for.

"I don't even know what it is," I said. "All I was supposed to do was make sure it was woven into the trailing edges of Between. They didn't say anything about it being half of a whole. It's not even *music*."

"Yeah?" Pet said. "You didn't know it was gonna have an edge to it?"

"Of course I knew," I said. "As I said before, it's supposed to be a subtle *buy more* vibe, not a thrall!"

Pet snorted softly. "It's subtle, all right. 'F'it makes you feel better, I don't reckon the thrall is in what you did. All the humans were already pretty well lulled when I got in here. That was the third thing I was gonna mention."

I may have breathed easier. "So, technically, I didn't do anything wrong."

Had I noticed how clear and stern those grey eyes were? Pet said, "It's still illegal, you know."

"I'm a hacker," I said. "I might only be half-blood, but I've got enough of my own power to avoid the human authorities." I wasn't sure whether I was offended and showing off, or arrogant and showing off. Either way, I wanted her to know that I wasn't someone who could be caught by a human.

"That's the problem," Pet said. There was a flare of annoyance to her nostrils, and it stung a bit more than I would have expected. "People like you—Behindkind—they don't obey our laws because they don't have to, and because there's no one to make them obey. If you're stronger than everyone else, you shouldn't use it as an excuse. That's when you need to make sure you obey the laws—when you don't *have* to."

I sank very slightly into my wheelchair. "I don't disobey human laws simply for the fun of it. There's a good deal of money in it for me, and no other work to be had for someone in my position. Besides, who in the human law is going to know what I do?"

"Yeah," said Pet. "And I didn't mean just *human* law, either."

My eyes flicked up to meet hers. I didn't swallow, but I wanted to. "What do you know about Behind law?"

Carefully unsaid, was the question *What do you know about the Troika?*

"Mostly what Athelas tells me," she said. "And I know that most forms of human coercion are still illegal by Behind laws, even if it's just to get a bit more money out of 'em."

"If they catch you," I told her. "And if they can bring you back. And if the courts don't sympathise with them. Humans can't represent themselves in Behind court, you know."

"That's if it gets to court," Pet said, and I was hoping that she didn't mean what I would have meant if I had said it.

I had another brief, unpleasant recollection of those human trader offices that had met with savage justice, and asked, "How do you know all of this?"

"I pay attention," said Pet. "You've heard about the Troika, haven't you?"

This time, I really did clear my throat. "They're just a rumour."

Pet grinned. "Is that what people say? Well, no wonder there's still some Behindkind willing to take advantage of humans. Still, you shouldn't do stuff like that."

"I really—" I stopped, and finished somewhat lamely, "I really did think it was just an inducement to buy more; something to keep the business profitable and keep a constant stream of humans in and out the door."

"Can you tell what else it's doing?"

I flipped my laptop lid up again and signed in.

"Hey," said Pet, in surprise. "How do you do that? Your computer just connected to the protection spell in here. Like it was wifi or something."

"The same way you access Between and Behind," I said. There was a lot more to it than that, of course—just like there was a lot more to bringing things that were Between into the human world. It was possible, but you needed to know how to do it, and not everyone could do it.

"What, so you use the computer as a kind of interface and just plug magic into the spell from there?"

I said, "Something like that." I had already been surprised by this little human so often that I couldn't bring myself to give into my curiosity and ask her how she knew the principles of Between magic.

"Cool!" Pet said, looking from myself to my computer with fascinated eyes. "You *are* actually hacking the magic! I wonder if Zero knows about this?"

"I certainly hope not," I muttered to myself. I didn't have the faintest idea who Zero was, but it was bad enough Pet knowing yet another thing a defenceless little human ought not to know. I had no desire to share the knowledge of my particular skills with another human—or any Behindkind, as far as that went. Not too many Behindkind knew about my skill set, and I preferred to keep it that way. I had enough work to keep me comfortable, and just enough anonymity to keep me safe.

"You can stop it, right?"

"It's my script and my program," I said. "I should hope so."

"Yeah," mumbled Pet, but her thin face was dissatisfied. "But I wanna know how you got through the protection spell, and I reckon Zero is gonna want to know how, too."

Whoever Zero was, I thought as I double-clicked into my program, he wasn't going to know if I had anything to say in the matter. The password screen flashed up at me and I typed a dash of symbols into the box.

An error box blinked at me.

"What?" Those clear, grey eyes were on me, uncomfortably shrewd. "Something wrong?"

"I must have typed my password incorrectly," I said, typing it again, more slowly.

"Ye-eah," said Pet slowly. "Bet you didn't, though."

The error box blinked at me again.

I typed the password a third time, this time a separate, distinct keystroke for each symbol, my jaw tight.

"Bet you," said Pet, far too cheerfully, "bet you it's not gonna work."

For the third time, an error box overspread the welcome screen of my program.

"It's not letting me in," I said. I sat back, nonplussed, and stared at my screen. We were as trapped as any of the humans in the café, and that made no sense, because I was *Behindkind*.

My stomach dropped. I was Behindkind, but I was Behindkind who hadn't yet been paid in full...

Pet, her eyes still sharp and on my face, asked, "They pay you yet?"

I laughed, and it sounded bitter. "Half. If they think I'm going to let them get away with this—"

Not that I could really stop it, unless I could hack back into my own program, which had so suddenly and mysteriously turned against me. I should really have had a closer look at that track they gave me before patching it in with my program...

And there was the issue of time, too—even if I could hack into the program, I would still have to do it before the music got to me, too. There was no one to miss me, no one to come looking for me— no one, unlike the humans with the Troika, to avenge me.

"I've heard music like this before," said Pet, musingly. "It sounds strange but familiar."

"So have I," I said. There was still a pit of dread in my stomach, but with it was another emotion I didn't readily recognise. A certain dryness to my mouth, or perhaps a lingering, unpleasant taste that shouldn't be left behind when I had coffee to drink.

It took a moment, but it came to me that it was disgust I was feeling. A faint but certain edge of disgust.

Across the table, Pet's wrinkled nose displayed the same sort of disgust. "Goblins," she said, wrinkling that nose even more. "Why do they always wanna mickey finn everyone?"

"I suppose you know all about goblins, too," I said. My voice sounded as resigned as I felt.

"Not much," Pet remarked. "Just every time I meet one, it's trying to drug me or knock me out."

"Goblins are like that," I agreed. Perhaps that was why, I thought, looking around at the Thralled humans, I felt so suddenly disgusted with Behindkind. It couldn't be any other reason: Behindkind were meant to prey on humankind, after all. There was nothing unusual or even exactly *wrong* with that—unless you fell into the hands of the Troika.

"What can we do about it? I'm slightly inoculated against stuff like this, but it'll get through to me if I'm trapped in here for long enough."

I filed away for later the question of how exactly a human was inoculated against Behindkind music, and said, "Glasses."

"What, like—" Pet nudged her chin at the waterglass stacks on the coffee counter. "—Like those?"

"Yes. With water in them."

"Okay," said Pet, rising to her feet with a readiness that was pleasing, "but why?"

I savoured that feeling for a little while; that oddly surprising feeling of knowing something that she didn't. "We can dampen the effect of the music with the water."

"Cool," said Pet again, with even more enthusiasm than last time. She called back across the café, "Is that because of the fae thing with water, or is it 'cos of the vibrations and stuff?"

I couldn't help laughing, and that made her laugh, too—a bright, cheerful sound.

"Yeah," she said. "I know weird stuff. Can't help it; I just keep picking it up here and there."

"Here and there as in *here* and *there?*" I called, with an amused look in her direction. If she said yes, I would almost believe her. Even though no Behindkind in their right mind would traipse through Between and Behind with a human in tow; even though no human could travel through Between and into Behind without help. I would still almost believe it, because she wasn't boasting, or teasing—she simply knew things she shouldn't know.

"This enough?" asked Pet, interrupting my thoughts. She had loaded a tray with half-full glasses of water, and now she staggered across the café toward me.

"Yes," I said hastily, ducking my head away by reflex as the tray passed a little too close for comfort. I was far from objecting to being doused with water, but if we would eventually be affected by the music, it was best to waste no time. It didn't escape my notice, however, that she had again avoided answering my question.

"Set them out around the outside of the booth," I told her. "Around the outside of my wheelchair, too; I can't hear the music all the time, and it can sneak up on me, too."

"Pretty handy, isn't it?" Pet said, laying out a semicircle of glasses. "All this stuff around, just waiting to be used. Reckon they wanted you to try and get out?"

I frowned. "I don't think so. Even if they didn't manage to catch me by surprise, they would have assumed I'd try to hack my way out without worrying too much about goblin music."

"Yeah, but you don't hear it properly," Pet said. "Reckon you would have decided you could hack your way out before it sneaked into your mind, too? Seems to me that the hope of holding out long enough to hack your way out would be a good way to distract you for long enough to be caught by the music."

"I don't know if I'll be able to hack my way out anyway," I said grumpily. "And if I do, it'll only be by the skin of my teeth. All this —" I waved one hand at the general, Thralled populace of the café, "will have to stay as it is. I might be able to give the two of us a way out, but I can't save them. The goblins'll be happy enough with that."

Surprised, Pet asked, "What d'you mean?"

"They're already lost," I said. I didn't want to explain to that big-eyed face that once we escaped from the café, each and every one of these humans would be lost to the human world completely. The only thing keeping the music from taking over completely was the last threads of the protection spell, which had woken to the danger of that load-bearing magic too late. Unfortunately, it was now also the thing keeping us in the café. I could have broken the spell that originally kept Pet from leaving, but Protection spells tend to take the approach that once the worst has happened, containment is the only safe procedure. I could already see the layers of it around the café now that it recognised the foreign, dangerous magic that twined around itself; it was drawing in on itself, tightening its hold on the café.

To Pet's expectant face, I said reluctantly, "To escape—*if* we can escape—we'll have to shatter the protection spell completely. No one will be able to get out, and it's unlikely that anyone will survive. The thrall spell in the music will turn inward for power, draining the humans to keep itself running."

"That doesn't work for me," said Pet. She grabbed two pots of pistachios from the counter and brought them back to our table. "Eat up and figure it out. If this thing is gonna turn on itself like a black hole, you'd better find us another way out. *All* of us."

I opened my mouth to protest, but Pet didn't give me a chance.

She asked, "Did it seem like they waited until I was in here to close off the exit?"

It was my turn to blink, then think. The timing had been, at the very least, coincidental. Pet was too regular a visitor to be unre-marked. At last, I replied, "Perhaps so."

Pet grinned. "Bit stupid, aren't they?"

If there was anything I'd thought about the goblins who ran the club below, it wasn't that they were stupid. But I couldn't help feeling uneasy, because it occurred to me suddenly that despite being trapped in a café with fifteen or so enchanted humans, Pet hadn't once shown any signs of panic—nor, if it came to that, succumbing to the same enchantment.

I drew in a breath through my nose, my fingers curling away from the keyboard, and turned in my chair to face her. "Who are you? Really?"

"I told you," she said. "I'm a pet."

"I thought you meant that your name is Pet."

She shrugged. "That's what they call me."

"Why did you say they're stupid? The goblins?"

"Well, 'cos of trapping you here without trying to immobilise you properly," said Pet agreeably. "But mostly 'cos of trying to trap me when they should know whose pet I am."

"Who—*whose* pet are you?"

"Well," said Pet, lifting her chin at the window, "*his*, for starters."

I followed her gaze, and let out an involuntary hiss, starting back in my wheelchair. There was a person there, his perfectly creased trousers and impeccably white jumper at odds with the dirty hostel wall across the road behind him. He could have been Korean or Japanese, I wasn't entirely sure which; but of one thing I was absolutely certain.

He was a vampire. Unlike human kinds, which are always difficult for me to tell apart, Behindkind are very distinct.

The vampire rapped on the window, his eyes half-lidded, and pointed at the door. Much to my relief, his gaze seemed to be focused on Pet. I absolutely did not want the attention of this very well dressed and extremely poised vampire. He already looked as though he was annoyed, and vampires aren't the most well-adjusted Behindkind at the best of times.

"What?" Pet called through the window. The loudness of her voice made me wince, but none of the Thralled humans around us so much as jumped.

The vampire's eyes flickered shut for a moment and then opened again with a distinct gleam of menace. He jerked his head at the door and said something that wasn't English. It could have been something like, "*Mun yolora.*"

"Can't," said Pet, turning back to the glasses. The liquid in some of them had already sunk; she refilled those, ignoring the vampire entirely in a way that brought cold chills to my neck.

The vampire thumped on the window with the side of his fist and jerked his chin at the door again, then turned his head on one side, his eyes narrowly on Pet.

She stuck out her tongue at him.

I coughed a laugh into my coffee before I could help it, and thought that Pet might have grinned across at me briefly.

The vampire bared his teeth and rapped once more on the window, this time with distinct warning.

"It's no good doing that," Pet called to him. "I can't get the door open."

"*Ku saramun—*"

"He can't open it, either. It's magic."

"*Ssulmo obnun saramiya.*"

Pet thumped the window with her clenched fist, startling me and the vampire equally. "Better than being a person without manners!"

"*Noh, Petteu!*"

"Oh shut up," grumbled Pet. "It's no good whinging at the window; something's gone weird in here and we've gotta fix things before we can get the door open. Why don't you make yourself useful and bring Zero here?"

The vampire shrugged and spoke again.

"Why don't you know where he is? He was still there when I left the house!"

"Why do you want Zero?" I asked, above the vampire's reply. "Is he someone who can help open the door?"

"Dunno," said Pet, frowning. "But he's pretty good at breaking stuff, so probably. He's usually around if I'm in trouble, so I thought he'd be here. Oi!"

I jumped, but she wasn't addressing me.

To the vampire, she said, "If you had a phone, you could have called him."

"*Nega wae?*"

"I didn't bring my phone with me. I was just coming out to get coffee for you lot!"

The vampire shrugged again. "*Nan obseo.*"

Pet thumped the window at him and yelled, "Get a phone, you old fossil!"

He fixed her with a black look and said something I couldn't understand. From the tilt of his chin, I guessed that he had said he *did* have a phone.

"Why don't you carry it, then?" demanded Pet, confirming my suspicion. "It's not like you lot can talk via telepathy!"

She made an annoyed sound, turned her shoulder to him, and said to me, "Sorry. It's only really Zero that's useful."

The vampire's eyes flashed, and I saw the snarl of two crossed incisors. He might not speak English, but he certainly understood it.

Perhaps he would have fulminated silently at the window if Pet had given him more attention. With her shoulder to him, he prowled across the footpath and leaned elegantly into a parking sign instead, his eyes dark and dangerous.

"Just ignore him," Pet advised me. "He's always stroppy. Funny, though—it's not his dinner tonight, so I don't see why he came looking for me. Want me to get a few more glasses?"

She jumped up and went to get them before I could agree, or ask what dinner had to do with anything, or even protest that I had no desire to be left alone with the vampire—with or without a good few centimetres of glass between us.

Failing that, I tried not to catch his eye. It's foolish to catch a vampire's eye in any circumstances, but this one was already significantly annoyed, and I had the distinct feeling that I was somehow exacerbating that annoyance to an unwise degree.

Unfortunately, as soon as Pet left the booth there was a flash of movement in my periphery. I looked up instinctively, to find that the vampire was watching me with his lips pursed.

I would have cleared my throat, but I didn't seem to be able to swallow. That amused him; at least, I saw his mouth curve up at the edge with malicious satisfaction, but there was absolutely no warmth of humour in his eyes. He displayed one wrist to the window, watch-face foremost, and tapped it lightly, one brow raised. Then he solemnly twitched that finger back and forth in the air, remonstratingly.

He thought I was taking too much time? But it had taken *days* of testing to have this hack catch on as it had, and I still didn't know why it had. Even if I could wriggle back into my program, there was no way I could dismantle the hack in a single morning, if I could dismantle it at all. I had no idea what had made it work correctly in the first place; or what the goblinkind had already had working in the background before my own spell took, for that matter. My goblinkind employers had been trickier than I had anticipated.

Perhaps the vampire understood my panic-stricken look. The other brow went up, and he traced one long index finger slowly across his throat, the pointed tip of one incisor showing from the lips that still curved with such a lack of humour.

I swallowed, involuntarily this time, and ducked my head to my work once again. If Pet had a vampire at her back, who else did she have? She had said *owners*, I was sure—and that Athelas she mentioned; who was he?

I opened my mouth to ask her about it when she came back with a carafe of water, but before I could, she asked, "Oi. Can they can see us in here?"

"They can," I told her ruefully. "There's a system I've been wanting to try out—"

Pet's voice was gloomy. "Bet you invented a magic-based security system and they paid you to install it."

"I did, and they did."

"Oh well, I reckoned you might have. Can they hear us?"

"No. I hadn't worked that part out yet."

"Oi."

"What?" I asked. There was a note of hope, or perhaps interest, in her voice. What had she thought of?

"If they can see us, reckon we better play with 'em a bit."

"How exactly can we play with them? If it comes to that, why do you want to play with them? I thought you wanted to get out."

"Yeah," said Pet thoughtfully, "but I reckon they know who I am, and I reckon they should know better than to try and trap me here. Anyway, I just meant that if we want them to think we're starting to be affected by the music we'll have to start doing things in a loop, sort of. Remind me to go get water again in five minutes."

"Ah," I breathed, my eyes lighting up. "So that they don't look too carefully while we're busy trying to get out, you mean?"

"'Zactly," she said. "Oi."

I couldn't help the hiss of laughter. "Yes, Pet?"

"Remember how you said you could only save us two, and I said you'd better find a way to save us all?"

For some reason, that made me laugh again. There was little enough amusing about our situation. "I remember."

"I s'pose you can't hack back into your program now that it's shut you out?"

My pride stung, I said a little bit shortly, "No. I'd have to get to the original program, and that's on my computer at home. If I tried from here, they'd notice as soon as I started fiddling with the system."

"Ye-es," said Pet, slowly. "Maybe we should try to call out, in that case."

"Call out?"

"Well, I can't get out to get help, so—"

"What help? How many more humans around here know about Behind?"

"Just me," Pet reassured me. "But if we can do a sort of internet call out, maybe Athelas can help from his side."

"I can do something like that," I agreed. "But I'll need to know where to make the, um...call."

"Like a physical address?"

"Is Athelas Behindkind?"

"Yeah—fae."

"Then a physical address will do."

"Hang on," she said, as if she'd only thought of it. "We don't have a computer at the moment. Someone sort of blew it up."

"It doesn't matter."

Pet looked knowledgeable. "Ah, is that 'cos you're using the bit of your computer that isn't really a computer to do it?"

"Exactly so," I agreed. I couldn't help being impressed and a little bit charmed. There was more cunning to Pet than her trusting and trustworthy face at first let on. It was pleasant, moreover, not to have to explain things—even if it was also slightly worrisome. "If he's at the physical address, I'll be able to contact him."

She glanced around the café suspiciously, then leaned in and whispered it in my ear.

For my part, I tried to pretend I hadn't committed it to memory as I mirrored my magic to my typing, and laid in the directions for the call out. I shouldn't really be thinking of anything but getting out of this café right now. It was bad enough that a pair of straightforward grey eyes had guilted me into doing things in a way that might see us all killed instead of escaping straight away and preserving at least my own and her life.

The protection spell, laced with my own hack and the goblins' ambient track, considered the spike of information-laden magic, and allowed it through. Just an outgoing call. Just a normal function of the internet.

"Good!" I breathed, as the outgoing connection sought and

found the right address. Now all I had to do was find something to attach the connection to—something or some*one*.

I could see him straight away, a single, powerful plume of Behindkind energy that crackled like lightening. I winced, but connected to it anyway, gasping when the strength of that fae touched the connection.

It seemed to me that someone said, "Dear me!" in a soft, interested voice; but just then, Pet said, "It worked!"

I must have been made of stone if I couldn't be warmed and pleased by the brightness of awe in her voice. My smile must have caught the vampire's eye through the window, because he looked coldly at me and smirked just slightly.

I looked away and back to the laptop screen, which now displayed a living room with two full, fat sofas and an old-fashioned, studded leather chair.

"Oi!" yelled Pet. "Athelas! Where've you got to?"

A murmuring of sound began to the edges of the vision, growing louder, then someone said, quite clearly this time, "Dear me! What trouble have you got yourself into, Pet?"

"I don't like the way you say that," Pet said, indignantly. "Actually, I've—well, I'm calling to see if you can help, so I s'pose that's fair enough. You know that protection spell Zero put on the café?"

A slender, middle-aged fae came into the frame, holding a teacup and saucer. "I do," he said. He looked very pleasant, unlike the vampire outside, and I felt, insensibly, relieved.

Then it struck me exactly what Pet had said. Her Zero had put in place the protection spell I had had such difficulties getting around?

"Yeah, well, someone paid 'Zul to hack it," she said.

"Marazul," I corrected her absent-mindedly. Good heavens! Who exactly was her Zero? And where had he gotten such ancient, powerful magic?

"Dear me!" said Athelas, a third time. "What an unfortunate

time for Zero to have left the house. He was in rather a hurry, so I didn't like to stop him."

It didn't seem to me that there was any particular meaning to the words, nor to the mild eyes that gazed at us, but Pet said, "It's all right. 'Zul is a friend. He's not holding me prisoner. That's the goblins."

"Can you not access Between?"

"She's a human," I pointed out. Of course she couldn't access Between. Even touching it—even—well, she had touched it earlier, but that was a vastly different thing to accessing Between. Touching Between was impossible, but accessing Between was *more* impossible.

Athelas ignored me, his eyes on Pet.

"Nope," she said. "Not for getting out; I already had a bit of a go. I can pull things through, but the protection spell has joined up with a thrall the goblins have started up. Reckon it doesn't want to let anything out."

"What a shame," sighed Athelas. "This is really Zero's field of expertise. I suppose Jin Yeong is there with you?"

"He's outside. Mostly glaring."

"He has been particularly sulky lately."

"That's what *I* thought!" said Pet, with the pleased air of one who has found herself unexpectedly in the right. Then, as if remembering her situation, she said rather more gloomily, "I suppose you'll just have to send Zero along when he arrives, then."

"I imagine he'll arrive soon enough," Athelas said. "Don't you?"

Pet, slightly annoyed, asked, "He's still got a tracker trace on me?"

"And isn't it a good thing!" said Athelas, smiling gently. Then he pinched the connection away from himself, away from the house, and let it go.

"Ow!" I said, my head jerking backwards.

"That was a bit nasty," Pet said, leaning forward to pat the apex of my head, where the recoil ached. "Sorry. Maybe I annoyed him this morning, too."

There was a tap from the window again, this one decidedly sharp, and Pet stuck out her tongue at the window. I ducked my head back to the level of my laptop screen, but I could feel the point of the vampire's glare. For the first time today, I felt myself utterly thankful to be trapped inside the café with a decent spell and strong glass between myself and the outside.

"Reckon they'd snap out of it if they were away from the music?" asked Pet, absent-mindedly drinking from one of the water glasses.

"In general, yes," I said. "The power of fae music is in its proximity."

"Pity we can't take everyone through the internet," she said. "Like calling ourselves out instead of just speaking to Athelas."

I stared at her for such a long time that she turned red and looked away, out the window. "Sorry," she muttered. "Athelas says I talk too much sometimes."

"No!" I said, suddenly and forcefully. "No! You're exactly right! It didn't occur to me—good heavens, I wonder if it's possible?"

"What? You can really send people through the internet?"

"No," I said again, and this time there was a smile growing on my face; big, bright, and wonder-filled. "But I think—I'm really very sure—you said you don't have a computer at home, didn't you?"

"Yep," she said gloomily. "Athelas sorta blew it up."

"What do you use when you want a computer?"

"The library. We sorta made a few adjustments to one of 'em."

I could have kissed her. "It's already fused with magic?"

"Well, sorta, I s'pose," she said. "Zero put a few protection spells around it, and I fiddled with the bit of Between that seeps through the shelves so that—"

"Perfect!"

"Really?" Pet sounded cautiously optimistic. "Well, I s'pose you know what you're talking about, but what good is the computer *there* when we're here?"

I spread my fingers over the keyboard of my laptop, smiling blissfully. "Because it's magic fused with electronics. And because it can receive magic that's pretending to be electronics. Like a batch of emails that aren't really emails."

This time it was Pet's turn to stare, and the admiration in her eyes brought a warmth to my cheeks I had thought I was past the age of displaying.

"You're gonna send everyone outta here through your not-computer disguised as emails?"

"That's right," I said, and I wondered if it was possible that I had ever felt so euphoric before. I didn't remember feeling this exhilarated, no matter how clever my hacks were.

Pet, grinning, rapped on the window and beckoned the vampire back over. He raised his brows at her, but after a moment where it looked like he was going to ignore her, he pushed himself away from the street sign and sauntered closer.

"Tell Athelas to go to the library and log in at our computer," she called through the glass. "We're gonna call him again. Got some email to send."

I HAD TOLD Pet that the goblins would notice if I hacked back into the system, but it hadn't fully occurred to me to wonder what we would do when they invariably noticed what else we were up to.

Pet must have been thinking about it for some time—perhaps even since I first made the observation—because when she came back with the latest carafe of water, she asked me, "Is that door the only way in and out of this floor from the one below? The one behind the counter, I mean?"

I nodded, busy with the ticklish little bit of magic that would soon be worming its way into my email.

"How long d'you think it'll take you? All of it, I mean—hacking the magic, setting up the email, and gathering all the people?"

I looked away from the screen in surprise, to see that Pet was half-beneath the table. "What, me? You want me to gather all the thralled people?"

"Reckon I'll be a bit busy," she said, in a muffled sort of way. "Ah! Got it!"

She emerged with two metal struts; they were twins of the ones that had been digging into my legs for half the day on this side of the table. As the sunlight from the windows hit them, they flickered and became something that was certainly neither as blunt nor as tubular as metal struts.

"Nice of someone to leave these hanging around!" Pet said cheerfully, casually feeling the balance of the twin short swords she now held.

"You can't do that," I said; which was ridiculous, because there she was, doing it—and there the swords were, fresh from Between.

"That's what everyone says," she said, even more cheerfully. "Don't tell anyone. I'm not supposed to show people."

"I'm not people," I said, with an attempt at coolness. "I'm mer."

That earned me a grin. "Anyway," she said, "I'm gonna be a bit busy, so you're going to have to get them all together."

I gazed at her stupidly for far too long, and then down at my useless legs. "I don't think I can. They're thralled; I can't round them up like cattle, and I can't force them to move, either. If I could walk, then *maybe*—"

"You have to," she said. "There's no one else, and I can't keep off goblins and round up humans at the same time."

"How—?"

"Dunno," Pet said. "But if you hack back into your program, can't you do something a bit different with the ambient track they gave you? Sorta pied piper 'em toward the right spot?"

Someone laughed, and it wasn't until Pet grinned back at me that I realised it was me. "Do you always verb your nouns?"

"I'm a scrapper, not a writer," she said, still grinning. "I don't have to speak properly. That mean you can do it?"

"Yes," I said, and there was still a laugh curling in my stomach because while I had been thinking of my shortcomings, Pet had been thinking of my abilities. No wonder she was pet to a fae, a vampire, and a Zero. "It's a pity you're already adopted. We work very well together."

Pet's grey eyes danced a little, but she only said, "I come in useful every now and then. You ready?"

"Nearly," I said.

Then I lowered my head and began typing magic into lines and blocks that grew until they moved and took on a life of their own, ready to do exactly what I needed them to do. When I had typed the second-to-last stroke, my fingers still poised over the keyboard, I paused for a moment.

I asked Pet, "Are you ready?"

She was by the counter—had been since she pulled those swords from the table, and I fancied I could hear the sound of something scratching, scratching, deep in the lower floor.

"I reckon," she said, without looking back at me. She stood easily, as if she'd always carried swords, her balance slightly to the back foot. I hoped she was as good with them as she looked holding them, because if the goblins got through her, there was no hope for the rest of us.

"If everything goes wrong, it's your fault," I told her.

She laughed. "Yeah, I hear that a lot."

But the tickling in my stomach was excitement, not fear. Had the human world always had such a warmth and life to it? I didn't remember feeling it before. The easy way to explain it would have been Pet's enlivening presence—bringing with it, as it had, danger—but that was too easy an answer. Something within myself had changed. Something within myself, after being so long used to pining for the velvet blue of Beneath, had grown to appreciate the sunshine of Above. At least for today, that sunshine was as beautiful as the blue of Beneath.

More, I felt alive. Or perhaps I merely felt that for the first time, I had a purpose that I could serve, even with a body that was useless no matter which world I chose to live in.

"Don't mind me," Pet said. "Things are gonna get noisy for a bit, but it's nothing I haven't seen before. Just do your bit and we'll be fine. I'm counting on you to get us out."

This time she glanced at me for the briefest moment, and I saw the trust in her face. That was a dangerous face for a pet to carry around with her. It was the sort of face that made people—that even made Behindkind like myself—want to be worthy of that trust.

"Here we go," I said. I started my dual-program running with the magic-laced press of a single button.

I'm not sure if the program or the goblin attack began first. I saw the closest of the café patrons twitch, his foot edging toward myself and my computer; and as he did so, there came the first slash of steel against steel.

"Get back, you ugly little needle-pusher!" said Pet, in a growl.

Something hit the wall behind me with a sticky splatter, and the high wail of a goblin battle-cry rose in the air, wild and savage.

I looked over my shoulder, unable to help myself, and saw Pet meet the onslaught of goblins with a competent, scything double sweep of her swords, blood arcing high to flower on the ceiling. The arms and legs that had been faunish and inclined to a likewise faunish awkward-ness were no longer awkward—lithe, quick, and beautiful, Pet danced forward and then back, the twin blades never still for a minute, her booted feet kicking away goblin needles, daggers, and teeth.

Something soft whispered by my arm, and I started badly, my wheelchair creaking. The first patron was at my right hand; his eyes were still clouded, but he stepped forward without prompting from me, and was caught within the influence of the second part of my program.

"Good luck," I told him.

I clicked the *new mail* button and the patron flickered slightly as the magic assimilated him. My finger hovered for just an instant longer over the mousepad, the cursor on the *send mail* button, but Pet was fighting for both of us at the other end of the café, so what else could I do but hit the button?

The patron vanished completely, and a moment later, the text at the bottom of my email client said *message sent successfully*.

I might have whooped.

"Good grief!" said Pet, her voice strained and just a little shocked. "I thought one of them had slipped past me! Working, is it?"

"Perfectly!" I said, relief blossoming bright and fragrant in my heart. I caught the next two patrons in the program—*new mail, send mail*—and they followed the first without a hitch.

Now this, I thought, grinning at my reflection in the computer screen, was what hacking life should always be. The delight of being always one step ahead of everyone else.

My fingers danced across the mousepad—*new mail, send mail*—and Pet swept the café clean on her side, until there was a kind of hollowness to the click of the mouse buttons, and Pet said from behind me, "They're gone."

I looked around in surprise to see who were gone, goblins or patrons, and found that we were entirely alone in the blood-soaked and magic-ridden café.

Pet threw the swords down on the seat next to me, where they made a sticky, bloody patch. Now that the time had come for our own departure, that patch of blood pointedly reminded me that there was a vampire waiting for me in the library—not to mention one Behindkind fae and, apparently, a Zero. What exactly would they say to my less-than-legal exploits today? It was very possible that they would report me, at the very least.

"Don't reckon they're game to poke their heads above the floor-line just yet," Pet said. She added encouragingly, "We'd better go now while they're still scared."

I let out a slightly shaky breath as carefully as I could. I didn't like to look like I was too frightened. "I may have misled you somewhat."

"About what?"

"I might have given you the impression that some of what I do is allowed under Behind law…"

This time, Pet really did look impressed. It was a sop to my bruised ego. "Flaming heck!" she said. "You're playing both sides, but in reverse."

"Not very clever of me," I said. "But it's a good living, and I don't particularly like either side all that much."

"Don't worry," Pet advised. "Zero doesn't care about stuff like that."

"Who is Zero, anyway?" I was beginning to feel, somewhat desperately, that this skinny, apparently friendless little human was backed by far too many people. A fae owner and a vampire owner were bad enough—what type of owner was this Zero?

"He's my other owner," she said, confirming that uneasy suspicion. "There are three of them."

"What's this one? Trollstock?"

"Nope," said Pet, without the kind of offence I would have expected from Behindkind, should I have said it to one. She added, "And don't think I don't know you were being rude, either."

I grinned. "That doesn't surprise me," I told her. I was beginning to think that nothing about this human should surprise me any longer.

"Anyway, you don't have to worry about them reporting you for stuff like that. Not if you're not doing wrong stuff with it, anyway."

Since this reassurance was paired with a slightly stern look that made it difficult for me not to smile, I said, "I certainly won't be doing anything like this again in a hurry."

"All right," Pet said, satisfied. "Oi. When we go through and the program stops, it's going to collapse on itself like you said, yeah? 'Cos there aren't any more humans to feed on?"

"Yes," I said. I had wondered if it would occur to her.

"Will it kill them? The rest of the goblins, I mean."

"I doubt it," I told her. "But it's possible, if they're weak enough."

She nodded. "All right."

"All right?" I was curious to know how she felt about that. I had known ruthless humans, and Pet wasn't one of them. She had killed in self-defence, but I hadn't seen any sign of enjoyment from her—just determination and a certain grim pallor.

"It's better than what Zero and the others would do to them," she said. "And it's time I took responsibility, if I'm going to be protecting people."

"Why should they be your responsibility? You said you're a pet."

"Because there's no one else," Pet said. "And there should be a human looking out for humans. You ready?"

"Ready," I said. If I had before thought her adorable and slightly unnerving, I now found that I respected her more than a little. "Hold tight."

"Yep," said Pet, and her voice was slightly breathless.

"Scared?" I asked, over my shoulder, smiling.

"Never travelled by email before," she said. "What about you?"

"Terrified!" I said, and clicked on the *send mail* button.

I HAD SAID I was terrified. Perhaps I even thought I was terrified. But when we rolled smoothly into the library, as safe and whole as if we had simply entered through the door, I knew real terror.

Because approaching through the shelves of books, a Between sword strapped crossways on his back, was Lord Sero—heir to half of the Behind world and leader of the Troika.

Blinding white hair, icy blue eyes, and a pale, severe brow I had seen last encircled by a band of white gold, danced before my dazzled eyes.

Zero? Her third owner, Zero, was actually Lord Sero?

He was so much bigger than I expected in real life, and so much icier. Looking up to greet him was Athelas—*that* Athelas?—his friendly smile no longer a thing to be trusted. Jin Yeong the vampire, his eyes malicious, cocked an eyebrow at me, but I couldn't find it in my dazed being to look away from Lord Sero.

"Who are you," Lord Sero demanded, "and why are you playing with my pet?"

Pet made a small, grumbling noise, but she said to me, "Didn't I tell you? It's pretty stupid of people to imprison other people's pets when they don't know who the owners are."

"That's Lord Sero," I said, resisting the urge to open the button that seemed to be choking me.

"Who are you," repeated Lord Sero, "and why are you playing with my pet?"

"He's 'Zul—"

"Marazul."

"—and before you start getting blood-ragey and majestic, he *is* the one who started the spell that sealed up the café, but he didn't know what the goblins wanted it to do. He didn't trap me in there, either; I did that myself because I thought it would be easier if one of us was in there."

"The advantage in one of us being in there, Pet," said Athelas, his eyes amused, "diminishes considerably when it's not one of *us*."

"Rude," said Pet. "I fixed it, didn't I?"

Lord Sero opened his mouth again, but to my astonishment and terror, she didn't let him speak a single word.

"It's no use saying *bad pet* at me, either."

Lord Sero closed his mouth, but his eyes narrowed.

Jin Yeong, his eyes dark and liquid, leaned over and bit Pet on the shoulder, lightly.

"Oi!" yelped Pet. She turned and glared at him, rubbing her shoulder.

"*Bad. Petteu*," the vampire said, very distinctly.

"If you turn me vampire, I'm gonna spend the rest of my immortal life pinching all your left socks!" Pet said, still scowling at him. "I'll make you so flamin' sorry you turned me that you hand yourself over for voluntary immolation."

The vampire shrugged and leaned back against a bookshelf. He radiated a faint smugness that was as irritating as it was subtle. It must have irritated Pet, too, because she stuck her tongue out at him again and turned her shoulder.

"*Anyway*," she said. "We fixed it, and I think that means—"

"There's no renegotiation of terms," Lord Sero said, without allowing her to finish.

"The Troika!" I croaked, feebly gripping the arms of my chair. I should probably have kept quiet while they were talking between themselves, but the words forced themselves out.

"Yeah," said Pet. "That's what Behindkind call 'em, anyway."

She rolled me forward again, and my hands frantically sought the wheel rims to stop a forward motion that only brought me closer to death.

"You didn't—you didn't tell me—"

"I did!" Pet's voice was indignant. "I told you that the goblins were stupid for kidnapping me because of whose pet I am."

"Perhaps you should *lead* with 'Troika' next time," suggested Athelas.

Now that I knew it was *the* Athelas, I felt as though I should have known from the start. Who else is called Athelas, with a soft, deadly gleam to his eyes, and is occasionally accompanied by a vampire? I hadn't heard any talk of a pet, of course, but it felt as though I could have pieced together that much at least.

"You said his name is Zero," I said, through numb lips. "That's Lord Sero."

"Maybe to you," Pet said. "To me, he's Zero. Oi. Where have all the people gone?"

JinYeong cocked his eyebrow at her instead. "*Saramdul? Musen saramdul?*"

She looked accusingly around at the three of them. "Did you let JinYeong eat 'em?"

"Jin Yeong is reformed," Athelas said.

"What, since last night?" demanded Pet. "He took a bite outta the trolley boy! I saw him!"

The vampire grabbed her by the arm and jerked her close, covering her mouth as his eyes flew to Lord Sero. I tightened my grip on the wheel rims to stop the rocking her swift passage created, and looked up just in time to see Jin Yeong release Pet again with a disgusted noise.

"Don't put your hand over my mouth if you don't want me to lick it!" she said grumpily.

"Well, perhaps *reformed* is going a bit far," Athelas allowed. "However, Zero saw the others out safely before they had a chance to notice anything else that they shouldn't notice."

"All right," said Pet, but she still looked suspicious. "Anyway, like I said, this is 'Zul, and he likes to be called Marazul. He doesn't like goblins much, either, and he hacks magic."

"Exactly how," enquired Athelas, his voice mild but his eyes distinctly unnerving, "did the two of you meet? I can't help feeling it was very...coincidental."

Pet looked slightly pink. "We both get coffee from that café," she said. "And it was the goblins who thought it would be a good idea to try and trap me too. They probably thought they could get a ransom for me. Stupid little twits."

"I see," said Lord Sero, looking down at her. "Perhaps a visit to that café will convince a few Behindkind of the danger of thinking like that."

"Don't think there's much of it left," Pet said. "And I killed quite a few of 'em when they were trying to stop us from leaving."

The vampire Jin Yeong showed his teeth for the length of a rather sibilant sentence.

"Exactly," Lord Sero agreed. "I don't like the idea of leaving stragglers. Besides, I'm interested to see what has become of my protection spell."

I swallowed as Lord Sero turned his gaze inevitably on me, his eyes thoughtful and just a bit considering. I didn't like that look. It could have been the look of a fae who was trying to decide how many limbs he should remove in case of hurt to his pet, or it could have been the look of a fae who was trying to decide how useful I could be to him. I didn't much care for either option.

"Don't go too far away," said Lord Sero. "We might have a use for you."

Oh no.

"There is certainly a use for him," Athelas agreed, those quiet eyes of his dwelling on me in a way that made me cold to the bone.

"I'm really very little use," I told them both, gripping the wheels of my chair on either side. "I'm not fully mer—I can't even swim beyond the light or remain beneath the waves more than five minutes."

"We don't have any use for a merman," Lord Sero said. "But we do have use for whatever you call this spell you've been fighting for the last couple hours."

"It's hacking," Pet told him again, helpfully. "Sort of magic, and sort of not. I didn't know people could do that sort of thing."

"They can't," remarked Athelas. His eyelashes had dropped a little, but I still felt chilled by his gaze. "That's why we're so very interested. I believe you'll have to resign yourself to seeing rather more of our Pet in the future—Marazul, was it?"

Lord Sero, with the slightest of frowns, said, "Yes. We'll discuss that later."

I had the feeling that *we* encompassed himself and me, not himself and Athelas. A little desperately, I said, "But your lordship—!"

"Don't worry, they won't hurt you," Pet assured me. "I'll make sure."

I looked from Pet's thin, waiflike frame to the whiplike Jin Yeong, and then further to the hulking mass that was Lord Sero, and felt a laugh bubbling up inside me. Best not to let that one out. I had the distinct feeling that it wouldn't sound quite sane.

"Later, we will also discuss your unique use of magic," said Lord Sero. "I want to know exactly how you got through my protection spell, and I *very much* want to know why you did it with my pet in the café."

"Oh," I croaked. "Well, your lordship, that's—"

"Yeah, all right, all right," Pet said. "Stop scaring him! He's had a pretty bad day and he's only been paid half of what he was owed. I'm gonna take him home now: you can ask him questions later."

She grabbed the handles of my chair again and wheeled me straight at them. Much to my surprise, not one of them tried to stop her; they each merely took a step back to avoid being run over. Athelas looked amused, JinYeong distinctly annoyed but aloof, and Lord Sero might have looked—was it possible?—slightly fond.

I saw it all in a startled flash, and then we were in the elevator and somehow outside the library, the warm summer sun folding around us. I took in a deep, careful breath, and let it out a bit more shakily than I liked. It occurred to me, not for the first time, that there was a great deal more to Pet than merely being the pet of Lord Sero.

It also occurred to me that given that fact, and the fact that she *was* Lord Sero's pet, it would certainly behove me to find a new place to live as soon as possible.

I COULDN'T SEE that Pet had any magic to her, but she pushed me up the road so energetically that it had to have been magic that kept her going uphill the whole way back to my flat. Neither of us looked too closely at the café as we passed; there was a blankness to the windows that was unpleasant, and I was glad that Pet kept us to the other side of the street.

"At least there's another café down the road," she said a little bit hopefully, as we approached my flat. "They do pretty good coffee, too."

"I seem to have lost the appetite for coffee," I said, gazing up at my flat. What a shame. I'd gotten so used to living here, and now I would have to find somewhere else. The goblins knew where to find me—worse, when Pet got back to them, Lord Sero would undoubtedly know, too. I was under no illusions that she wouldn't tell them everything they asked. She was their pet, after all.

"Oh," said Pet sadly, and I looked over my shoulder at her. "Does that mean I won't see you anymore when I get coffee?"

I was tempted. For just a moment, I was very tempted. It was a long time since I'd seen a look like that from a woman, human or Behindkind. And she was such a nice little thing, too. It could be nice to get to know her little by little, over a cup of coffee, with a smile.

But there was too much hazard to my life to be sitting quietly for coffee and smiles—and if there was too much hazard in my life, there was an overabundance of it in Pet's life. The kind of overabundance that spills over into the lives of those around them.

And then there was Lord Sero. I had seen the frown when he looked from myself to Pet, and it wasn't the sort of frown I would have associated with mere fondness for a pet. I didn't think it was a romantic interest, but it was certainly *something*. I could still feel that newness of zest to my life that I hadn't felt in years, and I wasn't prepared to end that at Lord Sero's hands if I made a mistake with his Pet—nor was I prepared to end it at the teeth of a vampire, if it came to that.

"I'll see you from time to time," I said, even though I knew it was a lie as I said it. I would be gone just as soon as I could pack my things. "They'll send you to ask me to do things."

"They will, won't they?" she agreed. "Athelas likes discovering new talents, and Zero loves using them. Don't be too afraid of them, 'Zul. They look mean—yeah, well, they are mean—but they look after their own."

"That will be more comforting when I feel that I am one of their own," I said, though I had no intention of being on such terms with the Troika. "They're not a particularly safe trio with whom to be on first name terms. They may be a necessary part of the Between world, but they're not a comfortable part of it. Perhaps when I know them a little better I'll be able to read them more clearly, but for now they're a midnight blue I'd rather keep away from."

That shade of midnight blue was the type that hid monsters in the deep with stars for eyes and spears for teeth.

"What about me?" asked Pet.

She asked it idly, but I knew the answer to that one straight away.

"You?" I asked, and found that I was smiling again. "That's easy. You're another shade of blue altogether. A deep, dark one with shiny patches that I didn't know existed."

Her face lit up, a brightness of happiness that brought the slightest tugging of regret to my heart. "I like that," she said. "It's not bad—being a pet, I mean—but sometimes it's nice to be something else."

I turned my smile up at her, hoping it wasn't as sad as it felt. "Then next time we meet, you'll have to tell me your real name."

"Yes," said Pet, and there was no sadness to her smile. As if she knew, better than me, that we would certainly meet again. "Next time we meet."

TIES THAT BIND

(You should be able to pick out exactly where in book seven this particular snippet occurs. In fact, it should fairly hit you in the face—like a book, hurled by a faintly smirking fae steward)

WHEN ATHELAS WENT TO FETCH THE PAPER THAT MORNING, there was a tie croaking at him from the welcome mat. If Athelas had had anything to do with it, there would not have been a welcome mat by the front door—in which opinion he had been surprisingly backed up by the vampire, who remarked that it made things too easy for any passing vampires.

The other two occupants of the house had remained indifferent to the risk. Zero, fae lord and Athelas' employer, no doubt had the right to a vote that counted for more than the other inhabitants; Pet, the little human he had adopted and kept around the house, should certainly not count for so much of the vote.

The business of the welcome mat aside, however, the fact that this tie was both familiar and croaking at him made Athelas shut the door rather hastily once he had seized his paper. He had been under the impression that this particular tie—now animate, mobile, and halfway between being a tie and being a frog—had been safely left behind in another place of residence. The pet had caused it to spring from one of the vampire's neckties in a fit of whimsy and revenge, and Athelas found its making and existence similarly troubling.

Nor did he particularly want it in the house, if it *must* exist.

In principle, Athelas approved of a piece of clothing that was capable of strangling its wearer. In practise, he was not sure that allowing Pet to make a pet of something else was the best idea—and if she knew the tie frog was once more in the house, Pet undoubtedly *would* make a pet of it.

He took a quick look out the window before moving back down the hall, and was very slightly relieved not to see the tie-frog any longer. Yes, it was certainly best if the pet didn't see that particular reminder of her own whimsy.

And speaking of the pet—she hadn't come down from her bedroom yet this morning. He had been waiting for a cup of tea before he started on his paper, but if things continued like this, he would have to begin making his own tea again, and that would be a shame.

The pet had a peculiar talent for making tea in just the way he liked it.

The creak of floorboards sounded above his head, and Athelas couldn't help sending a quick look up at the ceiling. He was rather sure that Pet was actually awake, but she had taken to staying above stairs much longer than usual over the last few weeks. It was sometimes difficult to gauge the Pet's motives for doing things, as they ranged anywhere from mischief to self-sacrifice, but he was quite sure there *was* a reason, and he would very much like to know what it was. She had left the house early yesterday and returned quite late with the smell of bridge troll on her, only to return to her own room to work on her contract.

If Athelas wasn't very much mistaken, she was also avoiding

Zero very slightly. That was, he thought, as he returned to the living room with his prize, both interesting and troubling.

Having returned to the room, he stopped short and sighed. The vampire had emerged from the shower while Athelas fetched the paper, and was at present lounging shirtless on the couch he shared with the Pet, one leg dangling over the armrest and surrounded by piles of books.

Athelas was at once assailed by two very different urges: one, to call Pet down at this moment to confront what she had unwittingly wrought; and two, to remind JinYeong very softly and quietly how very much Zero would object to his current state of undress and the reason attaching thereto.

Zero was, of course, perfectly well aware of the state of JinYeong's heart, such as it was. Athelas had watched the inevitable crumbling of said heart with both cool interest and a certainty that it would not be allowed to go as far as it had gone—a certainty that had been proved wrong. Zero did nothing more than warn— perhaps he expected JinYeong to do as he was told—but he certainly knew.

Even the banshees, hiding behind the stairway bannisters to hurl pistachio shells at JinYeong whenever he was otherwise occupied, knew.

In fact, arguably the only person in the house who *didn't* know was Pet herself.

The pet, Athelas reminded himself, sitting down. Not Pet. He was very good at making sure some thoughts stayed soft while the others were loud and easily heard, but it was better to keep his mind in order altogether. There was never any knowing when someone would come along to dust out the corners of his mind and shake out the cushions for crumbs. Far better that there be no crumbs to find —or at least, only the ones he wanted found.

He engaged himself with the paper, ignoring the files he had been reading earlier and smiling faintly at the headline stories— explosion in a café in North Hobart, group amnesia outbreak at the

Hobart Library coinciding with a major energy spike—but looked up when Zero emerged from the alcove he sometimes used as a study.

Athelas saw the quick upward glance his lord sent toward the staircase, and tapped one finger lightly against his lips. So Zero was wondering about the pet, too. Enough so that his first glance was toward where she could reasonably be expected to appear instead of the sight of Jin Yeong, shirtless on the couch and surrounded by books.

It couldn't distract for long, however. Jin Yeong turned a page, and Zero's cold eyes flicked over him. The vampire studiously engaged himself in his current book.

"Get dressed, Jin Yeong," said Zero, and continued through the house to the hall stand, ignoring the small snarl that pulled at Jin Yeong's lips.

Jin Yeong's eyes, stormy and dark, did not waver from the printed page, and Athelas was assailed anew by those two urges that would each have an entirely different consequence. Perhaps fortunately, he became aware of a faint, clothy slapping from the direction of the kitchen, and rose, swift and silent. He crossed the living room at his hunting run and entered the kitchen just in time to see the tie frog make a leap from the open kitchen window to the island bench in the centre of the kitchen area.

"I think not," he told it, dangling it in front of his face by two fingers. If it had had eyes, he would have locked gazes with it to show it he meant business, but it had no such appendages. No use wondering how it managed to map its surroundings, of course: items of whimsy very rarely worked by the usual rules of the worlds they inhabited.

Since he couldn't stare it into submission, Athelas merely tossed the tie-frog back out the window through which it had entered and closed that window with a touch of repelling magic to discourage it from coming back again.

That done, he filled the electric kettle and started it boiling with the hope that the sound would draw the pet out of her bedroom to brew his tea. Zero was still in the hall when he stepped down into the living room again, running small touches of magic down the flat of the sword that was pretending to be an umbrella in the hall stand.

Athelas wasn't surprised. The sword had vanished without warning some time in the preceding months while Pet was out, and again yesterday while she was out. One didn't like to jump to conclusions, of course, but there was certainly something odd happening, and odd things around this house almost always did involve the pet.

JinYeong was still scowling and pretending to read by the time Athelas returned to his seat, but his urge to needle the vampire had vanished with all the speed of the tie frog and possibly the longevity of that disappearance.

"May I suggest that lounging around the house half-dressed will not be conducive to your end goal?" he said as he sat down, instead of either of the more nuclear options that had occurred to him earlier.

JinYeong looked up from his book, stared at Athelas coldly and said, "I am beautiful."

"The pet," said Athelas gently, picking up his paper once again, "has seen many beautiful Behindkind."

The vampire's mouth grew a little sulky and almost opened—to insist, no doubt, that *he* was the most beautiful of them all—but pressed itself shut again. He said, instead, indicating the novels around him with a soupçon of irritation, "The book covers—"

"—are, one would suggest, designed to appeal to a different kind of female than our pet. Another woman would no doubt find your state of undress attractive—the Pet, I believe, is rather too well acquainted with your personality at this point."

One of JinYeong's brows went up, and his chin tilted. He was thinking, however, and when the thoughtful look had completely replaced the challenging one, JinYeong rose and padded away to his own room, emerging again in a soft silk shirt of muted green to throw himself back on the couch. In deference, one presumed, to the supposed better knowledge of romance book covers, that shirt was not buttoned up as much as it might be, but it seemed unlikely that an actual fight would break out with Jin Yeong now technically clothed.

The vampire had barely settled himself in again when the pet trotted down the stairs, braiding the last of her hair as she came, a hairband between her teeth.

"Heard the jug," she said, removing the hairband to wrap it around the tail of her braid. "S'pose you lot want tea and coffee and breakfast?"

Athelas waved the paper at her in a languid fashion. "It is a pet's job to fetch these, is it not?"

Pet gazed at him for a few moments with her head on one side, grey eyes dancing—trying to decide what he meant by what he said, as usual—and at last said obliquely, nodding at the newspaper, "You know you can get those online?"

"You heard the kettle?" countered Athelas. He wondered if she had heard anything else, or if she really had come downstairs after merely hearing the kettle boiling.

"You and Blackpoint should have a word," she said. Athelas would have liked to have known if she was ignoring the question or merely sticking to her own point. "Reckon you'd get along real well. And maybe he could teach you how to interact with modern technology."

"Thank you, I'm sufficiently acquainted with Blackpoint," Athelas told her. "However, considering what he did to the computer upstairs, not to mention Jin Yeong, I think we'll have to ask a few questions of that merman friend of yours rather shortly."

To his amusement, the pet's cheeks grew warmer in colour. She said, "Oh yeah? Reckon he can help with Blackpoint?" and turned to enter the kitchen with a very creditable casualness.

"I should think so," he replied, watching her shadow until it, too, disappeared and all he could see was the flickering of light as she passed by the kitchen window.

He withdrew his gaze, smiling, to find that he was being watched over the top of a book by a pair of dark, liquid eyes.

"You irritate me," said the vampire coldly.

"The feeling is entirely mutual," Athelas assured him affably.

"Reckon I should try to tell that human group about where the bridge troll was?" called Pet from the kitchen. "And other thinner places like that where it's easier for Behindkind to get through?"

"It would certainly free us up for more important things," agreed Athelas. "My lord? Do you have a preference?"

Zero appeared by the kitchen entrance for a moment, and Pet's voice said, startled, "Heck! How long have you been there?"

"You can try," Zero told her. "But I'm not sure they'll talk to you again."

"Me either," said Pet gloomily, appearing beside him. "I'll text Abigail; even if she only reads the text, she'll know. Then she can decide what to do about it."

Zero nodded and as Athelas watched, laid his hand on her head briefly.

Pet flinched a little—almost as if she had begun to shy away but stopped herself in time—but allowed the pat on the head, and Athelas felt a faint tickle of amusement.

He met Zero's eyes and saw in them the same question that was in his own mind, but the other fae looked away quickly enough and went back to the hall, leaving Athelas to his thoughts.

This was new, and potentially interesting. There were at least three or four reasons he could think of that would cause the reaction he had seen, and Zero's reaction to Pet's subtle flinch had rid his mind of two of those. The pet certainly was a scintillating housemate.

She returned to the kitchen before he could return his gaze to her face, and he heard the collection of small rustles and clinks that meant Pet was gathering together the tea tray.

Athelas was not quite sure when he became aware of it, but there was a niggling at the back of his mind as Pet came back into the room. The very faint gibbering of banshees became audible a moment later, and Jin Yeong frowned, looking away from his book.

He opened his mouth to direct a question at Athelas, but shut it again when Pet sat down beside him and peered at his stacks of books as she set the tray on the coffee table.

"Good grief!" she said. She looked as though she was trying very hard not to be horrified. "What are you reading those for?"

"I believe that Jin Yeong is conducting a species of inquiry into the female mind," Athelas explained to her, flicking a glance toward the staircase. "Human female, of course."

"What, through those?" Pet went through the stacks, swiftly and ruthlessly. She said to Jin Yeong, "You'll only get a very partial insight if man-chest covers are all you stick to. Where did you get these, anyway? They have library tags, but you can only get out ten books at a time."

"The librarian was verrrrry helpful," said Jin Yeong, looking at her unblinkingly over the top of his book.

Pet grinned. "Female, was she? All right, at least she got you a few others—there's a few classics in here as well as the man-chest, so you'll get a bit of variety. Didn't she tell you that there's different kinds of romance?"

A slight tug to the house set off one of Athelas' boundary magic spells, and Zero said from the hallway, "Athelas?"

"Right away, my lord," Athelas said, which made the pet grin.

"You two are as good as a show sometimes," she told him. "All hidden signals and double-speak. You could do a stage show like that. Oi. Are these *all* romance?"

"*Ne*," said Jin Yeong precisely, as Athelas rose once again and strode toward the staircase.

There was certainly a disturbance upstairs, and loth as he was to think it, the most likely cause of it was—yes, there it was, just hopping out from the upper living room doorway. The tie frog, as smug as anything made of cloth and magic and mischief could be.

Athelas took the stairs swiftly and silently as Pet argued, "You can't just read romance if you want to get insight into the female mind! We care about other stuff too, you know! Anyway, you're always biting women—why don't you ask them?"

Jin Yeong's tones were sulky. "They cannot answer properly when I am biting them. I am a distraction too great."

"You're a mosquito, you mean," Pet's voice said, without mincing matters. "Oi! Are you all right up there, Athelas?"

Athelas, who had leapt for and just barely missed the tie frog, took a moment to steady his voice before he replied, "Certainly. Do pour out, Pet; I'll only be a moment. I trust there are shortbreads?"

"Got you some special ones," she said.

She was a good pet, thought Athelas, making another dive for the tie frog.

He missed. It was certainly getting faster, and it had by now gotten the idea that he was not willing to allow it into the house. As mischievous as Pet, and every bit as determined, it seemed as though the tie frog was set upon seeking out its maker. Athelas caught it with a touch of sticky magic instead of by hand, and escorted it out by the window through which it had evidently gained ingress; an impressive feat, considering the fact that the window was open a bare centimetre.

Had the pet really been sneaking in and out again, then? He'd thought that she had recently become secure enough in her position in the household not to need to do so. This was certainly the same trick she'd used when she was hiding in the house, however; one might wonder exactly what it was that had led her to start sneaking out again.

One did, in fact, wonder.

When he returned to the lower living room, Pet was going through Jin Yeong's stacks of books while he alternately objected, pretended to be reading, and hung over the edge of the couch to jealously observe which of the books she was spiriting away into which piles.

Athelas picked up his teacup and the file he had been going through that morning—now perilously close to the pet, and assuredly *not* safe for pet consumption—and sat back in his chair. The movement made Pet look up at him, her grey eyes bright and sharp.

"Still looking in odd corners for our murderer?"

"Always," murmured Athelas, resisting the urge to hide the file. The pet would certainly notice—she had a terrier-like nose for discovering things that would be better not discovered—and he fancied it wasn't yet time for her to go over that particular set of documents and reports. Instead, he crossed one leg over the other and coolly opened the file to sort through its contents. He was already quite well aware of the contents, but he had too much respect for the pet's nose for trouble to do anything else.

It also seemed good to him, as he was sipping the last of his tea, to enquire of Jin Yeong, "And what has your reading hitherto taught you of the effects of biting stray women—or perhaps pets?"

Pet gave vent to a small, deep chuckle and said, "That's just business, though, isn't it? You need blood and you have to bite to take it. There shouldn't be any effects that aren't covered under *side effects of vampire spit.*"

Jin Yeong stared at her. "My bites," he said frostily, "are *soft* and *warm* and—"

"If you start talking about how warm you are again, I'm gunna—"

"Athelas," said Zero from the hall, in a voice that rumbled and couldn't be ignored. "I'd appreciate it if you took a look at this."

Athelas closed his file and put it tidily beneath his teacup on the coffee table.

"A bite is not a transaction!" snarled Jin Yeong. "Would you say a kiss is a transaction?"

"With you, it is," Pet said, as Athelas rose. "Sometimes I need extra speed and strength, and you need to not feel like I'm gunna die every five minutes. Of course it's a transaction! What else would it be?"

JinYeong's eyes widened in outrage, sparking a small, amused delight very deep within Athelas where it couldn't be seen without careful digging. He crossed the room in the warmth of that amusement and heard the vampire still spluttering behind him.

"With me? With *me*? *Yah! Noh!* Who else are you kissing, then?"

"There's something wrong with you," said Pet's voice with finality, softening a little as Athelas passed into the hallway.

Athelas found the eyes of his lord already upon him, and came to a leisurely halt in front of him.

"Are you," asked Zero, his voice as cold as ice, "encouraging or discouraging JinYeong?"

"In general, whichever is the most amusing in any given circumstance," Athelas said. There was real ice in his lord's voice, and for very good reason, but Athelas was also quite well aware of the humour there, too. "Are you suggesting that I should cease to bait the vampire? Or are you perhaps irritated by my twitting of the pet earlier?"

There was a brief pause where Athelas was quite sure Zero was swiftly working his way through to the safest answer. At length, his lord said, "I won't concern myself with the pet's crushes unless they threaten our standing. JinYeong, on the other hand, shouldn't be encouraged: he's already unstable and I strongly disapprove of—"

"Yes, my lord?"

"—of whatever it is that's going on in his head right now," Zero finished, with an exasperated tone that suggested he was very conscious of how weakly he had finished the sentence.

"I was under the impression that encouragement was a stabilizing force, my lord," he explained. "Amongst other...influences."

"Were you," Zero said, the certain grimness to his tone making a doubt of the question.

"Certainly, my lord. JinYeong does seem rather more...

predictable in his wildness these days. Are you saying you wish me to cease er, encouraging him?"

"Don't bait me, either," advised Zero, but there was a cool shade of amusement to his eyes. "I still haven't decided whether it was encouragement or discouragement."

"You suggested that you might care for assistance, my lord?" Athelas reminded him gently. Zero was holding the heirling sword, and there was certainly something odd about it; there had been something odd about it ever since the pet picked it up and brought it into the human world with her.

Zero frowned, his attention elsewhere. "I've a feeling it will have to wait. Perhaps you could tell me why there's a...disturbance in the toilet room?"

At the same time, Pet's voice said, "Oi! There's something fishy going on in the toilet!"

"It is a toilet, not a fish-bowl," muttered Jin Yeong, as she got up and trotted toward the back of the house.

Athelas sighed, and set swiftly across the room in an attempt to mitigate the almost certain defeat, but when he caught up with the pet, it was already too late: she had pushed open the hanging door and was in the act of tipping up the edge of the seat with one careful finger.

To Athelas' faintly horrified startlement, the tie frog was clammily attached to the bowl of the toilet, hunched under the toilet seat like any normal frog might have been.

Pet made a small, explosive sound of laughter and said to it, "There you are! I've been looking for you!"

"Really, Pet!" he expostulated, but it was certainly far too late.

"Don't worry," she said cheerfully, removing the tie from the toilet bowl. "I'll wash my hands—and the frog, too. Can't let it go hopping around in the outside world for people to see, can we?"

"I fail to see why it should hop around the inside of the house, either," Athelas said, making one last, feeble attempt at ridding the house of the nuisance before it really took hold. "It would be far better off outside and more frog than tie—or turned back into a tie."

"Heck!" said Pet, sounding startled, as the tie frog attempted a hasty, long-legged leap through the doorway. She caught it and murmured, "No, don't worry, I won't let them turn you back into a tie!"

Athelas sighed faintly. She was already crooning at it. "Very well, Pet," he said. "But if you must keep it in the house, you'll need to take care of it."

"What, you mean you're not gunna feed it and take it for walks?"

She was grinning in a most reprehensible manner.

More coldly, Athelas said, "I shall certainly not bother myself to take care of it."

"Yes, dad," she said.

"Becoming attached is a very bad habit of yours," he said to her, with a three-fold layer of meaning. "You should fix that."

And the pet, who had understood every layer, still grinned back up at him once more, and said, "*Yes*, dad."

WATERMELON IN THE MOONLIGHT

(This story is outside the bounds of the City Between continuity. I wrote it before the Big Reveal of book eight and couldn't find a way to slot it back into the continuity of the series without substantially changing it. So enjoy it with all the comfort of someone who has never read book eight, and for whom the events thereof never happened—an alternate timeline, if you will, where our happy, murderous little family is still whole)

THE MORNING OF THE DAY BEFORE JULIA'S FINAL EXAMS, THE watermelons in her backyard turned vampiric. Perhaps it was even the night before that. Whenever it happened, it was sure that there was already something wrong with the watermelons when Julia went out to refill the bird-bath.

Yawning, she ran the hose desultorily over the surrounding garden bed after filling the bird-bath; it was then that she noticed something odd about the watermelon patch. Her hand faltered on the trigger nozzle, and the spray dribbled away to nothing as she frowned at the patch. She didn't remember them having strands of deep, blood-red through the rind like that, and she had watered this part of the garden last night.

Julia stared at the watermelons, mottled with red and green in an almost offensive parody of Christmas colours, and wondered what had gone wrong with them. It wasn't just the almost veiny threads of red that clawed their way through the green patches, it was the random tufts of feathers that Julia had assumed to be merely itinerant left-behinds from a particularly fierce neighbourhood cat, but on closer inspection turned out to be dead birds—whole, bloodless, and very, very dead.

Crouched beside them for a closer look, Julia shivered. Then she saw the dead cat that was shrivelled and bloodless in the very centre of the watermelon patch beyond them, and uneasily stood once again. Who had been killing cats and birds in her backyard last night? Why were there so many of them? Why were they right in the middle of the watermelon patch?

And had that watermelon vine just moved?

Julia took a couple of hasty steps backward and went back into the house, looking over her shoulder as she went.

That settled it. She needed to get more sleep as soon as her exams were over: she was getting paranoid and delusional. Imagine thinking that the watermelon vines were reaching out to her just because she was creeped out by dead things in the garden.

Still, Julia couldn't help looking out the window from time to time as the morning wore on, and by eight o'clock, she was trying to convince herself that the watermelons hadn't grown in size and that the vines weren't closer to the house.

But by nine o'clock, the watermelons were closer to the house, and they *were* bigger. If Julia wasn't mistaken, there were also more patches of dead things in there, though she never looked out at the right time to see whatever caused that to happen.

Julia made herself a cup of tea and sat down by the back window to keep a suspicious eye on the garden out there, though she wasn't sure if she really wanted to see it if something *did* happen.

Nothing untoward had happened this morning, she was quite sure. Last night, though: last night had been weird. Next door had been weird last night, and if Julia were to assign blame to anything or anyone purely on instinct, she would have blamed next door. Next door was always a bit strange, but never in a quantifiable way —unless you could count three older men living with a college-aged girl as strange.

If she thought about it for too long, it grew stranger. Or perhaps it was just that her mind seemed to want to remember more odd things than she could quite account for having seen. But Julia was on her third year of a nursing degree and had no time to think about anything but her studies for too long, which was both convenient and comforting. She had the strange, not-quite-thought that if she thought about Next Door Things too much, life would get dangerous in a way that she couldn't quite quantify.

She vaguely remembered seeing people come and go, but she'd only been living in the house for half a year now: the real estate agent had mentioned that her house went through a lot of tenants when she signed the contract, but Julia hadn't much cared. The carousel of tenants probably had more to do with the way the kitchen was falling apart and the sagging eaves than it did anything next door.

In fact, if Julia were to think about it objectively, she couldn't see any real reason to blame next door at all. But something had happened last night, hadn't it? She slid her fingers around her mug of hot chocolate and sat back, eyes glazing.

Last night. Last night, Julia had been watering the garden in the muggy twilight, wishing it were a bit cooler, when something had smacked into the fence from the other side with enough force to crack the wood and bow it inward. It was a sickening kind of sound, and the wash of liquid that sluiced under the fence, flushed red with the sunset, was just a little too thick to immediately make Julia think of water.

She froze, then started across the lawn with the stunned

thought that she was going to be called upon to triage someone who had somehow been thrown across a yard and into her fence. A sudden cool, unseasonal breeze sent a chill through her bones as she approached the fence, and Julia shivered, wondering if she could hear groaning or if it was just the moan of the wind in her ears. As she got closer, something scrabbled against the fence, and a young, vaguely familiar female face appeared. There was the dark hair, huge grey eyes in a thin face, and the pair of squarish shoulders that were just starting to look elegant instead of angular.

The uni student next door, realised Julia, with a premature sense of relief.

"Sorry 'bout that!" the girl called, slinging her arms over the top of the fence in a casually friendly way. "We were messing around and *someone* started throwing stuff against the fence."

"It was an *accident*," said a cold voice, and another face appeared over the wooden palings. It was another student—probably—this one male and Korean, by the looks. He was beautiful, and although his voice sounded not-quite-right, Julia couldn't help smiling at him. He turned an accusing look on the girl and added, "You should have let me deal with it in the house."

"I *just vacuumed*," she told him with finality. Julia had the impression that she had said something similar many times in the last few hours. Of Julia, she asked, pointing, "Oi, can you chuck us that little medallion?"

Julia hesitated. Looked down at the still moving pool of what *had* to be blood puddling toward her white sneakers. Started to reach down for what she assumed the girl meant by *medallion*—a silver-tone celtic knot on a silver chain that had evidently been flung over the fence at some stage and was now only inches from the tide of blood—and then hesitated once again.

"That's—that looks like blood," she said, tilting her chin at the puddle. "Is everyone all right over there?"

The uni student looked at her with wide eyes. "Nah, that's not blood. That's definitely not blood. See, if it was blood, there'd have to be a dead person over here. That'd be *too much* blood."

"*Too much blood*," said the Korean student beside her, his eyes warm and brown and his voice still not quite right. Julia had a vague feeling that he might not have said the exact words she heard, but she was quite sure they were true.

She wasn't quite sure what else he said, but she yawned, because the evening suddenly seemed tiring, and she had been studying for too long today.

"I mean, this amount of blood would be enough for two va—er, people," added the girl.

Julia already knew that. She was too sleepy to wonder why the uni student next door knew it, and the more she looked at it, the more it seemed like it was just rusty water, not blood. By the time she could bring herself to crouch and dip a finger in it and draw it out again, she could see that it really was rusty water, the rust separating from the water visibly in the last light of sunset.

"Right," she said, retrieving the medallion just before it was subsumed by the moving puddle of water. "Can't be blood. That's crazy. Oh, right, I'm Julia, by the way."

"Pet."

"Sorry, what?"

The woman grinned at her. "The name's Pet."

"Oh, short for Patricia," Julia said vaguely, passing the medallion over the fence.

Pet reached for it, but the Korean student stretched out a hand and took it instead. "Short for something, anyway," she said, leaning on the fence again. "Thanks for that: sorry about the noise."

Julia found that she had already almost forgotten about the noise. What had it been, a scream? A body hitting the fence? But no, it couldn't have been either, because that liquid was rusty water, not blood.

"That's all right," she said. "What happened, anyway?"

"We had an unexpected, um, guest," said Pet. "He's gone now."

Julia didn't quite like the way she said it, but it was all right, because the liquid still trickling its way through her garden and right into the watermelon patch was only rusty water. Nothing to worry about.

Instead of asking the bothersome question about where the water was coming from, Julia found herself asking, "You studying somewhere around here? I'm in my third year of nursing: exams in two days."

Pet seemed to think about that for a moment before she said, "I mean, yeah, I s'pose you could say I'm studying."

"Exams?"

The Korean student said something soft and warning, then turned and went back to the house.

"Sorry, what?" Julia said.

"He says that it's a full moon tonight, so you should be careful."

"Careful of what?"

"Not a clue!" said Pet cheerfully, looking over her shoulder at the other student. "He says weird stuff sometimes. He explains stuff more than the other two, but he's trying to be mysterious and cool at the moment, so who knows when he'll unbend enough to explain himself. See you 'round: good luck on your exams!"

What had Pet known? wondered Julia now, coming out of her drowsy memories of yesterday evening to find that her tea was cold. More importantly, the watermelon vines were *definitely* closer to the house, and the same coils of veiny red that she had seen digging in across the surface of the watermelons themselves were corded around the vines themselves.

The vines which now, Julia saw in horror, had plucked the neighbour's cat from the top of the fence where it had been stalking birds, and drawn it back into the watermelon patch. She made a vague, distraught protest and sprang to her feet, her cup of cold tea tumbling from her hands as she darted for the kitchen with one thought in her mind.

The gas-lighter was in the top drawer where it always was, and it lit when she pinched at the trigger with a shaking finger. Perfect. Julia turned and ran for the back door, snatching up the jerry-can of mower fuel as she ran through the hall, the gas-lighter in her other hand. She fairly leaped through the door and cleared the few patches of vines that coiled to trap unwary feet, dashing for the watermelon patch, but the next door neighbour's cat was already dead, a sad, soggy little patch of fur to add to those already in the garden.

Julia stared down at it in a mix of nausea and rage, and threw a wild arc of petrol over the whole patch from her jerry-can. It was already far too late, or course: the vines uncoiled from around the cat as she watched, soiling the garden soil with blood. More importantly, those watermelon vines were already beginning to move toward her. Julia threw another smelly arc of petrol over the patch and laid a trail behind her as she swiftly made her way back toward the house, rage in her heart.

It was a bit of a wobbly trail over the parts where she had to jog and leap over vines, but it ran all the way to a foot from the patio stairs, and when she was done, Julia threw the still half-full jerry can back toward the watermelon patch. It sailed through the air and spluttered down within a few inches of the garden.

Close enough, thought Julia, and reached out a surprisingly steady hand with the firelighter. She heard the *click* as she squeezed the trigger, though she didn't seem to remember actually squeezing it, and there was a faint breath of silence before everything from three feet and beyond went *whoof!* and exploded into a sheet of flame, hot and oxygen hungry in a way that seemed to draw the breath from her lungs.

She turned on her heels and ran for the house again, slamming the door behind her just as an explosion of vine and leaf and flying watermelon flashed by the kitchen and sun-room windows simultaneously; giant vines, monstrously larger than they had been a moment before, were slithering around the *entire house*.

No! How had the fire made the vines *bigger? How?*

Julia's nerve broke. She ran for the front door, hoping desperately that she could make it through to the road before the vines got her, too. She tumbled through the door and almost collided with two people on her front patio as the watermelon vines stretched and reached for the road, scaring off a small terrier that had been sniffing at Julia's mailbox.

She caught herself with a shriek, then uttered another wordless cry as a vine tried to wrap itself around the waist of the girl from next door. Pet. What was Pet doing here?

And why did she have a teapot?

Julia wasn't left wondering for long: Pet threw the teapot at the closest watermelon, which was, ridiculously, just by the stairs, and the Korean student smacked the soaking watermelon smartly with a wooden broom.

The melon exploded in chunks of red, and the vine withdrew, sharp and urgent.

"Borrow a cup of sugar?" Pet asked breathlessly, as watermelon vines snaked around each other behind her to make a lattice around the patio.

Julia said wildly, "If you think I'm going to believe you just want sugar when there are watermelon vines trying to grab people off the streets and off my patio—!"

"Fair," Pet said. "Well, you'd better invite us in, then. This is Jin Yeong, by the way."

"Invite you—invite you *in*?" Julia stared at her. There was still a slight chance for a very quick person to make it to the street before the watermelons could shut in the whole place, and she didn't want to miss it.

"Well, we're gunna be sucked dry if you leave us out here, and I don't reckon you wanna be left alone with vampiric watermelon, do you?"

Julia's jaw dropped. By the time she had gathered herself, Pet was already edging past her, though Jin Yeong waited for her weak,

"Come in, then," before he stepped through the door. By way of a joke, she said, "What, I suppose you're a vampire, too?"

"Yess," he said, in a thoroughly satisfied way.

"What do you know about vampires?" asked Pet, in an accusatory sort of way.

"Well, you just said the watermelon are vampiric, and they've been feeding on the birds and—and the cats," Julia told her, feeling sick and rather accusatory herself. "That *was* blood yesterday, wasn't it?"

"Told you," said Pet, with the grace to look faintly guilty. "We had an unwelcome guest. I didn't know that it could cause trouble on a full-moon night, though: Jin Yeong explained this morning when we um, realised that something was going wrong. It would have been fine if it hadn't been watermelons or pumpkins, mind you."

"We have come to rescue you," said Jin Yeong, as if he expected to be congratulated.

Julia looked him up and down, taking in the slender beauty of his figure, the impeccable style with which he was dressed, and the very carefully arranged hair.

"I think we should have made a run for it," she said, chewing on her lip.

"Not much good doing that," said Pet. "You'd just have vampiric watermelon overrunning the neighbourhood, and there go all the kids and animals."

Julia hadn't thought of the rest of the neighbourhood: she had thought only about escaping. Pet's surprise made her feel guilty.

"I didn't mean that I want people to die," she said stiffly. "I just thought that—"

"Good grief, I'm not *blaming* you," the other girl said. "No, this lot is our fault, anyway. We sorta seeped into your garden; it's not like you knew anything about it. Running away is good sense in most situations, apparently. Oi—you got a really big kettle or something? I haven't got me teapot anymore, and it was too small, anyway."

"I've got—I've got an urn, if you want it? It's for the uni, but—wait, why do you want an urn?"

She was talking to the air: Pet had already vanished into the kitchen. Julia might have followed her in there, but there was something very forbidding about the kitchen doorway that stopped her in her tracks. Instead, she turned an uneasy look on the vampire Jin Yeong.

"Is she—does she know what she's doing? What is she doing?"

"I do not know," said the vampire, with a look of dark amusement, "but it will be *verrry* enjoyable. It is always enjoyable."

Julia shot him a distinctly uneasy look; she didn't care for the relish in his voice when combined with the bloody look to his eyes. "Looks like you two know each other pretty well," she said. She didn't know her next door neighbours at all, and she rather regretted having to know them now, but she was curious.

"Yes," said Jin Yeong. "I will marry her."

"That hasn't been decided!" yelled Pet, from the kitchen. "Don't tell people we're gunna get married! I haven't even agreed to date you!"

"I am beautiful," Jin Yeong said to Julia, with absolute certainty. "She will change her mind."

"I don't think she cares much about looks," Julia said, without thinking about it. If Pet had cared about looks, there was a big, glorious white-haired bomb-shell next door as well: slightly on the older side, but Julia liked an older man. Jin Yeong was certainly beautiful, but he was on the slender side, despite the tautness to his frame that suggested he was both strong and muscled.

"Yes," Jin Yeong said again, this time darkly. "It is very irritating."

"You're very irritating," Pet retorted, emerging from the kitchen and wheeling in front of her an urn that was much larger than Julia remembered hers being.

No, she realised, with a buzzing in her ears; Pet wasn't wheeling it in front of her, it was *trotting* in front of her on four little black legs that shouldn't have been moving, let alone in a self-governing sort of way. And the urn, instead of being a small, metal thing of about two feet in height, was now a monstrous steel canister that puffed a small stream of steam behind it and towered over even JinYeong, who was the tallest in the room.

Julia sat down suddenly in the closest chair and then sprang hastily to her feet to avoid being burnt by the urn as it turned uncertainly around the room as if unsure whether or not it would stand on someone's toes.

"Go on," Pet said to it encouragingly.

The tea urn tapped its feet in a little, joyful circle before it evidently decided that *yes*, it *had* been given permission, and toddled toward the back door, tooting a bit of steam out from the bit of the lid that wasn't quite sealed properly.

Gaping and not quite breathing properly, Julia said, "*What* did you do to my urn? And *how?*"

"It's been wanting to move around for a while," Pet said incomprehensibly. "I just encouraged it to be a bit bigger before it started moving around: it's gunna spray some hot water at the watermelons for us."

"How do you know?"

"It told me," said Pet, and threw something at her. "Here, you'll need this."

Julia caught the item in a self-preserving kind of reflex, and found that she was holding a broom. "What?" she said weakly.

"Well, Athelas and Zero are out," Pet explained, tossing another broom in JinYeong's direction. "But JinYeong knows a bloke—well, a vampire, actually—from the Balkans, and it's brooms."

"What's brooms?"

"Just go out and hit as hard as you can at any watermelons," Pet said, her hand resting on the knob of the back door. The urn did a little dance in expectation. "With the brush end if you can manage. Try not to panic too much, but if you really have to, try to panic *toward* the watermelons, right? And only go for the ones that the urn has sprayed already."

"Why?" asked Julia. "Why can't I go for ones that haven't been sprayed?"

"Because they will kill you," said the vampire, turning a look of exasperation on her.

Julia wondered why she had thought his eyes were warm yesterday. "There's no need to be rude," she said resentfully, and followed Pet toward the door.

The vampire muttered something that she couldn't understand, but Pet said soothingly to him over her shoulder, "All right, no need to get your knickers in a twist. I know you were only trying to answer the question: you just gotta work on your delivery. You lot ready?"

"Ready!" said the vampire, with a gleeful chuckle. "Open it!"

Julia didn't have a chance to say that she wasn't ready—wouldn't ever be ready to go into battle against vampiric watermelons under cover of a far-too-large tea urn and armed with only a wooden broom—because the door was open and the vampire and the urn had vanished, and now Pet was turning to go, too.

One last, encouraging smile, and she was gone.

Julia gripped her broom handle with whitened fingers, and realised that Pet didn't really expect her to come along. She had left her here, safe in the house, but with a weapon in case the watermelons got in.

She very nearly didn't go out, either. A breath: then two, and three, and four, passed. And Julia knew then that if she didn't go, she would never go. Never go, never be able to face the terrible unknown, never be worth the price of her education or her pride as a nurse. If she couldn't do this, how could she ever hope to be a nurse?

"I don't have time for this!" she said in despair. "I have exams!"

And she dashed out of the back door after Pet and Jin Yeong.

She caught her breath in terror when she tumbled down into the backyard from the patio stairs: above her, vast, serpent-like coils of vines writhed, around her burgeoning watermelon swelled, red and green and hungry, and seemed to lean toward her. She saw the quick figure of Pet smacking watermelons with the brush end of her broom; she heard the sickening crack as they split into bloody chunks. The urn, flashing silver and green in turns, spurted boiling water and steam, and closer by, JinYeong darted back toward Julia.

"Ignore the vines!" yelled Pet over the sinuous sound of vines writhing and the shriek of the urn. "Get the watermelons—bash the little beggars!"

Julia did as she was told, wildly, viciously, eyes slit almost shut, but she felt only the solid, painful reverberation of her broom ricocheting off tough watermelon without anything of the effect that Pet had had.

She stopped, almost panicking, and JinYeong fairly threw her sideways as a watermelon vine slashed out protectively. It hit him instead, and he went flying, but he seemed to be used to it because he flipped in the air, gracefully, and landed on his feet like a cat, smashing a watermelon that was too close to Julia for comfort.

"Be careful," he said, pressing down on her head.

Julia dropped to her knees, obedient to that pressure, and a stream of boiling water spurted over her head. She rose when JinYeong did, battering steamed watermelon with the brush end of it, and by the time they had cleared that side of the house, there was a fresh lot of sluggish, parboiled watermelon to smash into bloody pulp while the hot, sweet scent of them hung in the air.

Her hands had seized up around the broom handle, and blisters had formed and burst long ago by the time Julia found that there were no more watermelons to smash. She spun in a shaky circle, her broom held aloft and trailing bloody watermelon, and JinYeong dodged and swore at her in Korean, brushing watermelon flesh from his lapels.

"Do not do that!" he snarled at her. "I am already untidy!"

"You can't blame her for the watermelons being messy," Pet said, turning in a far more considered circle than Julia had, her grey eyes running competently over the entire yard for signs of further danger. "Looks like that's it, doesn't it?"

"What if they come back?" asked Julia, breathing too heavily and ignoring Jin Yeong's complaints.

"They won't," assured Pet. "You only got 'em this time because there was vampire blood *and* a full moon *and* watermelons. I mean, you can pull up the whole bed, but you don't really need to."

"My suit is *messy*," said Jin Yeong severely.

"You got stuff in your hair, too," Pet told him, removing chunks of watermelon flesh from his hair. He stood perfectly still for that, and even ducked his head to make it easier for her. He also stopped complaining, and when she was finished, Pet said brightly, "Right, that's the lot. Reckon it's about time for a cuppa, don't you two?"

The tea urn tooted at her and trundled back toward the house, and Julia, still feeling charred and shattered and sick, said, "What?"

"Coffee," the vampire said, grinning a far-too-toothy grin at her. "We have won. Now it is coffee time."

"We almost died!" Julia called after them, entirely flabbergasted. "We almost died! What do you mean, it's time for coffee!"

"Coffee tastes better after you've almost died," Pet said exultantly. "You'll see!"

"I should be studying," Julia said helplessly. She had said the same thing about ten or fifteen times now, but she was as well aware as the other two evidently were, that she would by no means be able to do any such thing. Who could, after fighting off giant vampiric watermelon with boiling water and wooden brooms?

The coffee might taste better after you had almost died, but Julia had always liked tea better, anyway.

"Tests tomorrow," said Pet, with a vaguely encouraging tone. "It's bad timing, but we can fix that for you."

"You keep saying that, but I don't see how you *can*," Julia said in despair, as someone knocked at her door. "Oh, what *now*? They haven't come back, have they?"

"Nah, that's more of our lot," said Pet. "Athelas and Zero, I reckon. I texted 'em. They're good at this sort of thing."

"What sort of thing?"

"Inconvenient things," Jin Yeong said to Julia, as Pet went to answer the door.

Julia might have taken offence at that, but she had the idea that he thought he was being helpful, so she tried to ignore the feeling that he was referring to her as one of those inconvenient things.

"What, like stress because vampiric watermelons try to eat you a day before your finals that you should be studying for?"

"Yes," said Jin Yeong. "And memories."

That would be nice, Julia thought gloomily. Get rid of inconvenient memories just like that: *poof*, there go the memories of impossible events that stopped one from being able to think or study or concentrate on anything besides the fact that one had almost died by watermelon that day.

She looked across the room and saw the huge, pale, almost glowing figure that was the white-haired hunk from next door, beside him a quiet, older man in houndstooth and brown shoes. Julia didn't spare the older one more than a moment of her attention: it was the pale, broad-shouldered one that always made her catch her breath.

When she could concentrate on anything else, Julia became aware that Pet was watching her. The other girl might have been grinning slightly.

"This is Zero," she said. "Zero, this is Julia. She tried to save a cat from vampiric watermelon and didn't die."

Zero looked as though he didn't quite know what to say. Cautiously, he said, "Well done," and that seemed to please Pet.

"Yeah, I thought so," she said.

"May one ask exactly how the watermelon vines became sufficiently large to reach the road?" enquired the older male. There was a slight smile in his eyes.

"I tried to set them on fire," said Julia, lifting her chin. "What do you want? Look, I need to study, and today has already been a nightmare, so—"

"They want to take away your memories," explained Pet.

"Oh, thank goodness!" Julia said in relief. She appreciated the fact that Pet and Jin Yeong had rescued her, but she was beginning to feel as though she couldn't even sit comfortably in her own house. "Look, I don't want anything to do with vampiric watermelon, and I have final exams tomorrow. I don't mean to be rude, but I don't have *time* to be stressed out by anything else, so if you can pretend not to know me after this—"

Pet surprised her by chuckling, low and delighted. Entirely without offence, she said, "Yeah, that's fair. All right, we can fix it."

"I," said the man in brown, "can fix it. You can make tea."

"Rude," said Pet, still quite cheerfully.

"Do sit back," the older man said to Julia. "Make yourself quite comfortable."

She obeyed him, soothed by his voice, but asked, "Why?"

"Because you'll stay like that for some time," he said. "Don't worry, you'll awake completely refreshed."

"Is this—is this something like hypnotism?"

"Goodness me, no!" he said amiably. "Now, how shall we begin?"

"Exams," Pet said helpfully.

"Oh, yes," said the older man meditatively. "You will do rather well on your exams, I think. You're a clear-minded young human. Very bright, well put-together. There's no need to keep on thinking about things that don't make sense, now is there...?"

JULIA WOKE, feeling more refreshed than she had in months. She felt so refreshed, in fact, that it took her some minutes to remember that today was Exam Day. When she did, the idea didn't bring with it the same kind of panicked uncertainty that it usually brought: instead, Julia felt the faintest tingle of anticipation.

Today, she faced the final challenge in her journey toward becoming a nurse.

That called for a cup of tea and a couple of chocolate chip biscuits for the ride to uni.

The urn seemed particularly warm and comforting that morning, though Julia didn't know why. She didn't know why she had chosen to use it instead of the kettle she also owned, either: perhaps it was just that it was there, and still had a bit of water in it when she came into the kitchen.

"You'll like it at the uni," she said to it, surprising herself. She wasn't the sort of person to talk to inanimate objects. "Lots of people there. They'll love you."

The urn puffed a bit of steam, and Julia found herself smiling. She was still smiling when she stepped out onto the front patio with her travel mug of tea.

"I'll do well," she said to herself. "I'm clear-minded. I have everything I need."

Then she stepped over a few, withered bits of watermelon vine that shouldn't be on the front patio, and headed off for the bus stop.

HOCKEY STICKS AT MIDNIGHT

(This story occurs after book ten; an Afterward in which Pet and Co are still working together for various situations, but which is also before the events of the following stories in this book)

THE HOCKEY STICK WASN'T THE FIRST THING TO DISAPPEAR—IT was just the first of Georgina's own things to disappear. It was brand new, still with the stickers on. Georgina knew it'd been there behind her door the night before, but in the morning, it was gone. It came back several days later, in the wrong place and dirty instead of shiny new.

No, first it was cricket bats. Georgina saw who took them—almost. She wasn't really there; just a shadow of a person who reached right through the car and pinched two cricket bats from beside Georgina.

"Hey!" said Georgina, but it was too late. The shadow person was gone, and so were the cricket bats. She heard later, at school, that someone found the cricket bats in an alley nearby, battered to pieces like they'd been used to destroy a car.

So when Georgina woke up in the early morning a year later to see the shadowy figure of a woman passing through her room, she sat up straight away. As she did so, the shadow woman reached out and took her hairbrush from the dresser.

"No!" said Georgina. "It's mine!"

The shadow turned hastily and caught sight of her.

Georgina said again, "It's mine! You can't have it!"

"Flamin' heck!" said the shadow, sounding impressed. "Can you see me?"

"Yes," she said, scowling. "Stop stealing my stuff!"

"Oh," said the shadow. "Sorry. Only I really need this."

"Why do you need a hairbrush?"

"It's not a hairbrush," said the shadow woman. "It's just pretending. It's actually a kind of net thrower. I think. I've never used one before, but this one wants to be used."

Georgina wasn't sure she believed that, but she asked anyway, "What was the hockey stick?"

"A really good scythe," the shadow woman said. "Someone I know knows how to use one."

"You took the cricket bats last year, too," Georgina reminded her. "Were they pretending to be cricket bats, too?"

"Oh, the cricket bats! Yeah, I had to fight a rock troll. They were just cricket bats, though—very useful. Were they yours, too?"

"No, just the hockey stick."

"Right. Did that come back all right?"

"It's *dirty*."

"Oh. Sorry about that. I'll ask Ze—someone to get you another one."

"That's okay," said Georgina. "It's still new, it's just dirty now." She looked up at the shadow woman, and came to a realisation. "You're going to take my hairbrush anyway, aren't you?"

"Yeah." The shadow woman sounded apologetic. "Sorry. But I need it. I'll bring it back."

"What are you fighting today?"

"Goblins, mostly. Oi. Don't go into your spare room when the lights are out, okay?"

"How come?"

"You've got a goblin problem, and if you can see me, you might be able to see them."

Georgina tried not to shudder. She'd already heard the scratching at night, though she'd never seen anything. It was one of those things that mum wouldn't believe—one of the things that mum thought was just an excuse for Georgina not to do her piano practise alone in that room.

"All right," she said. "You can have the hairbrush."

"Ta," said the shadow woman, and she disappeared.

Georgina settled back in her bed, hugging her knees. It wasn't until the faint sound of high-pitched wailing floated into her room, accompanied by some softer *thud*s, that she curled back under her covers, smiling, and went back to sleep.

<hr>

TALKING SHOP

<hr>

(After book ten. We're into uncharted territory now, you blokes: here be monsters)

SOMETHING WITH TENTACLES WAS WAITING FOR DERRICK WHEN he stepped out of the corner pizza shop and onto Murray Street. He had started up the hill in the direction of the library with a steaming box of pepperoni pizza that pleasantly scorched his fingers, his thoughts slowly unwinding with the warmth of that prospective meal, when it happened. He had had a hard day's work and it felt as though the pizza warmed the chilled part of him that always froze to ice by the end of the day.

He always got too emotionally invested in his work—he knew that—but he couldn't really help it when his work involved kids. Derrick had found out that a hot pizza did a lot to take away the chill that came after one of his busier days, and this particular pizza shop was one of his more frequent visits even though he knew it was dangerous in his line of work to go to the same place too often.

He had expected that perhaps one day someone would be

waiting for him, but he'd never expected tentacles instead of someone. It wasn't as though he didn't believe in tentacles. While in Derrick's experience tentacles were a far-off and unconsidered fear that should exist either safely in the ocean, or safely on someone's dinner plate, it would have been difficult to ignore the fact that there were tentacles existing in the world.

It would have been hard to ignore these tentacles, anyway: wet, pink with agitation, and very, *very* large, they unfurled from the alley with hypnotizing slowness before his eyes and then curled back in again, this time around him.

Derrick might have been ashamed of the scream that tore out of his throat if he'd had a moment to feel anything other than the blind fear that made him duck, dive, and then dash across the road without checking for traffic or stopping for the pizza he'd dropped. He would have gone down the alleyway into the Hanging Garden if he'd been able to get his brain to think; instead, he found himself fumbling at the handle of a cream-painted doorway without any idea of how to open it, or why he was opening it, except that he was in danger and this doorway felt safe.

Somehow he managed to pull down instead of across, hands shaking, and all but fell into the shop, shutting the door behind him and putting his back to it with an almost uncomprehending look around.

Buttons, said his brain. *Buttons, buttons, buttons.* That didn't make sense until he dragged a breath into his lungs and tried to look around again. His fingers automatically found the lock on the door and turned it as he did so, and he found himself gazing around at rows of buttons, trim, and scraps of fabric. He was in a sewing kind of store.

Why had he come into a sewing kind of store? There was nothing here that could be used against tentacles that existed where they shouldn't exist. Derrick, with ghostly tentacles of fear crawling up and down his back, still had to take a moment to remember how to breathe before he could try to push away from the door.

He expected the ghostly tentacles to become real ones any moment—expected them to burst through the glassy door and snake around him to suck him back into whatever demesne they originated from. Then, with sweat on his brow, he heard the muffled thump as heavy, wet, tentacles, now bright orange, hit the door and explored its glass-and-wood surface. The door shook at his back, sending a crawling terror shivering down his back and the sweat springing up on his brow.

The door shook. Derrick shook.

And yet, somehow, the tentacles didn't seem to be able to break through the door. Derrick didn't know why, but he felt a sudden resurgence of the feeling of safety that the shop door had given him from the first, and wondered if he had simply been lucky, or if he had been somehow able to innately sense that this was the one place in which he would be safe.

Whichever it was, now that he was in here, he was certainly not going to leave again if he could help it. Not until he figured out why there were tentacles in Murray Street—or at least, why they were after him in particular. There shouldn't be tentacles in Murray Street, but the most disconcerting part of tentacles in Murray Street was the distinct feeling that those tentacles were after him in particular.

Derrick looked around the store once more, jumping as the tentacles hit the door again, and found that he had seen only a part of the store: there was a corner up ahead, turning the shape of the shop into an L. That looked promising.

He left the door and rounded the corner in a hurry, as if the tentacles had eyes that could see through the glass of the door, and stopped short with a sweaty tingle running across his scalp. There was someone behind the counter ahead of him.

He took another moment to breathe; having done so, he realised that it was just a girl behind the counter—not very old, maybe twenty or so, and with only one arm. He was well aware of the importance that the edge of being male, large, and older gave him in this situation, and he felt it with all the relief it deserved.

"What can I help you with?" the girl asked, leaning with her one arm on the counter. Her voice was friendly, and very slightly louder than he had expected.

"I'm here for my first day," Derrick said. Whatever it was that was stopping Tentacled Thing from coming into the shop, he needed to take advantage of it until he could figure out what was going on and what was trying to kill him. He very much doubted he could do that by telling this girl that he was trying to escape a giant squid.

"Reckon you've got the wrong place, mate," said the shop girl thoughtfully.

"This is number 777, isn't it?"

"You're half right," she said. "We're 777b. You probably want 777a."

"There is no 777a," Derrick said bluntly. He could feel sweat starting to pop out on his forehead again. At the very least, he wanted to know if there was a door out the back, through which he could escape, if the front door stopped being as effective as it had been against tentacles until now. "I would have seen it. Look, I was told I had a job here—you're supposed to be giving me the tour and showing me the ropes so I can start tomorrow."

"Yeah?"

"Yeah." And since that didn't seem to be enough to bring her around the front of the counter or invite him around behind it, he added, "I can call the boss if you want. They probably aren't going to be really happy to be disturbed at this time of day, but that's on you. They must have thought I'd be a good replacement for you if they didn't tell you anything about it."

That got her moving around the counter, and Derrick let out a slightly shaky breath. He was very good at finding just the right kind of pressure to get people to do what he needed them to do, and it was in that moment an almost heart-stopping relief to find that he hadn't lost the knack.

"Sounds legit," she said. "We'll have to have a bit of a chat. What d'you reckon?"

She looked slightly to the side of him instead of directly at him as she asked the question, and Derrick, still vaguely numb from the experience of tentacles around his waist, experienced a muffled sort of shock to find that there was someone standing next to him.

That someone was gorgeously suited, immaculately brushed and combed, and had what seemed to Derrick an unpleasantly sharp, white-toothed smirk in a dusky-skinned face. Made more foreign by the gleam to his eye than the Asian features, he was such an unexpectedly unsettling sight that it took Derrick a good thirty seconds to realise that the words being spoken in his direction weren't gibberish.

When at last that fact made itself obvious to him, it was as if the radio dial had slipped into exactly the right notch. He heard the man say clearly and without any muffle, "I will taste his blood just *once*."

Derrick felt a chill spread from his neck and up into a web behind his ears. That chill made him forget about pretence and applying pressure and left only the simple facts in their place. "I need...I need help," he said. "I can't go back out there right now. Someth—I mean, someone is waiting for me."

"You coulda just said that," the shop girl said. She sounded reproachful. "Or pretended that you needed a suit—it takes a good while to measure up and pick out styles and fabrics. You didn't have to try and push me around."

"Something with tentacles is trying to kill me," Derrick said, pushed to the ropes. She wouldn't believe him anyway. "I didn't have time to think of the best way to infiltrate the shop—I was just trying not to die!"

"Yeah, that's fair. What sort of tentacles are they?"

"What sort of—wait, you believe me?"

"I mean, it would have been easier to believe if you were up at the seafood place in Elizabeth Street—that's why I asked what kind of tentacles they are. There's a kraken somewhere up there. We don't have one here in the business district and they don't seem to migrate much, though, so I reckon this is something else."

Derrick took a dazed moment to wonder exactly what kind of tailor shop this was, right on the streets of Hobart, before he said, "I think a kraken would have been bigger."

"That's what I thought," the shop girl said triumphantly. "You don't really get away from a kraken—well, not without losing a bit of bodily integrity, anyway. I didn't think we got giant squid around here, but there's always something new popping up around town."

"I shall bite him to make sure," said the assistant with the unpleasantly sharp teeth, as though he had been quietly proceeding with his own line of thought while the conversation went on around him.

"I don't—I don't want to be bitten!"

"Nobody wants to be bitten," the shop girl said reasonably. "Oi, stop gnashing your teeth at people, you oversized mosquito!"

"I am not oversized," said the assistant. "I am Fun Sized."

"Give him one bag of snack chocolates, and that's all you hear," the shop girl said, shaking her head. Of Derrick, rather suddenly, she asked, "Why is something with tentacles chasing you?"

"That's what I want to know!" he said. "I didn't even know tentacles were a thing that could happen—how should I know why they're after me? Do people usually know?"

"Not usually, no. I just thought you might have an idea; you seem a bit more put together than most people are in this sort of situation."

"I wouldn't have been this much put together if those tentacles had gotten hold of me before I got through the door," Derrick pointed out. "Why couldn't they get in, by the way?"

"Oh, this is a special door," said the shop girl. "I made it to be pretty strong. I had to coat it with a lot of—well, I suppose you can think of it as the glue that sticks the worlds together—to make it that strong."

"Don't you mean "the world"?" He wasn't sure she did, but he would have liked to be sure that she did. Derrick had the feeling that one world was more than enough for him right now.

"Don't worry about it," she said, a bit too cheerfully. Less hearteningly, she added, "It's probably safer if you don't know about it anyway."

Derrick opened his mouth to say that in that case, he'd much rather not know, when someone knocked on the door. It was a very polite knock, and it didn't sound like a tentacle, but Derrick still jumped.

"Don't let anyone in!" he said, as the shop girl took a few steps around the corner to see what it was.

"You said it was tentacles," pointed out the shop girl. "That's a man."

She was right, but Derrick still had that hunted sort of feeling that anything outside the door at this point was likely to be Trouble, and he had already had his fill of Trouble for the day. He tried to grab for the shop girl's uninjured arm when she headed toward the door, and snatched his hand back at what was definitely a snarl from the assistant.

Today, of all days, he wasn't sure that the shop assistant *wouldn't* bite him.

Instead, anxiously, he followed the shop girl with the assistant following him, to make sure that she wasn't about to do something stupid—like open the door. That door was presently quite a bit more opaque than it had been earlier, but he could still see through it enough to recognise the figures of a shortish man, and a woman beside him. As they got closer, it became easier to see, and by the time that the shop girl and Derrick both stopped in front of it, the glass was very nearly completely see-through again.

That meant that Derrick was far too conscious of the unsettling hazel eyes that immediately flicked over to him and wandered over him for far too long, assessing.

"What do you want?" demanded the shop girl, when it became apparent that the couple outside the shop were more intent on looking than talking.

"Yeah, we're gunna need to take him with us," said the man, pointing at Derrick as if there had been any doubt about whom he was talking.

"Why?"

The simple question seemed to delight the man, and he looked at the shop girl properly for the first time. "I'm a bounty hunter!" he said, as if that made the matter any clearer.

Derrick, still confused, felt two tiny pinpricks of pain in his shoulder, and hunched away defensively from the dark shadow at his shoulder, which turned out to be the Korean assistant. That assistant stepped back at the same time, licking what appeared to be blood from his lips.

"Did you...did you just *bite* me?" Derrick demanded, aghast.

"This is human," said the Korean man. He sounded disgusted. "What else would I be?"

The bounty hunter echoed gleefully, "What else would he be?"

Derrick met the bounty hunter's eyes through the glass and felt a prickle of challenge—or fear. There was something not-quite-right but slightly familiar about the way the man looked at him, and Derrick didn't care for the feeling. Besides that, the bounty hunter looked...not quite sane. Derrick wasn't sure if it was the light stubble across the lower half of the man's face, or the slightly-too-long, dirty-blond hair that had been gelled and swept across his head in a haircut that wouldn't have looked out of place in a production of The Great Gatsby. Despite the fact that he was a head shorter than Derrick and a couple of centimetres shorter than the woman who stood by his side, he managed to exude a vaguely unhinged sense of menace that only grew the longer he stared at Derrick.

At last, to Derrick's relief, those disturbing eyes moved away from him and fixed on the shop girl instead. "He's our prisoner. Well, he was going to be, anyway."

"I'm not your prisoner!" yelled Derrick, thumping the glass. "I don't even know you!"

"He's human," said the shop girl, as if that explained everything. "You can't have him."

"Oh," said the bounty hunter. "Well, I suppose we'll have to come in and get him, then."

"Good luck!" said the shop girl. "It'll take more than two bounty hunters to get through my door."

"I'm not a bounty hunter," said the woman outside. She seemed indignant at the thought. "I'm just a secretary."

The shop girl grinned. "Bounty hunters have secretaries?"

"I'm not *his* secretary."

"She's a spy!" said the bounty hunter happily. "Look, it'd really be a lot easier if you just let us in, or sent him out. He's not a very nice person."

"I don't even know you!" protested Derrick, once more. It was rude of someone who had something to do with tentacles to tell people that he wasn't a very nice person—particularly when he didn't even know them.

"We're not letting anyone out without a lot more information," the shop girl said, and that made Derrick a bit indignant, too.

The cheek of it, suggesting that she'd send him out if there was enough information to warrant it! The idea made a cold shiver run down his back: what did a one-armed girl who was far too blasé about tentacles consider enough information to send him out to what seemed like probable death?

The shop girl and her assistant, decided Derrick, now cold to his ears, weren't to be completely trusted.

"Sorry, can't give out information!" said the bounty hunter. "Here we come!"

The door went inky black, cutting off sight of the outside world.

It wasn't until the shop girl said indignantly, "Oi!" that Derrick looked around and saw that all windows had had the same dark transformation.

The only reason he hadn't noticed it at once was because the lights in the shop were on, and very good. Those lights were also not quite...natural, if Derrick was right. He didn't waste time staring at them in concern, because the black door and windows were more concerning.

"*Igae mwoya?*" complained the assistant, and somewhere in the back of Derrick's mind, where it shouldn't have been, popped up a meaning of "*What is this?*"

"Is that...is that the squid's ink?" he asked, breathing too fast. "There were tentacles out there, and now everything's gone dark. Are they playing with squid ink? *How* are they playing with squid ink!"

"I mean, they *could* be, but I doubt it," the shop girl said dubiously. "For one thing, we're not underwater—heck, we're not underwater, are we? Nah, I would have felt it."

"I didn't say anything about underwater," Derrick said, feeling more worried than before. The world had changed in strange and terrifying ways since this afternoon, when he had walked home after a big day feeling as though he knew how to work everything, and how everything worked. "How could we be underwater?"

The shop girl and the assistant exchanged glances before the shop girl said—reluctantly, it seemed to Derrick— "The world isn't exactly the way you thought it was this morning. And it isn't just one world—it's three."

"It is trifle," said the assistant. For some reason, it felt as though it was the first time he was really speaking in English, even though Derrick had understood him earlier.

The shop girl grinned at him. "Yeah, it's like trifle. The human world is the cream and sprinkles and chocolate curls, and the world Behind is all the jelly and savoiardi biscuits—or sponge cake, if you want—where Behindkind and things with tentacles live. The custardy bit in the middle is Between—and since it's soft…"

Derrick understood vaguely. He said slowly, "Stuff gets through?"

"Stuff gets through."

"Stuff like tentacles?"

"Yeah, amongst other…things."

Derrick's brain churned for a few moments before he asked, "How do you know about it? The Between and the Behind and the…Behindkind."

"One of the things that got through killed my parents," she said.

"Can you use the Between bit to do things? Since it affects the human world?"

The shop girl blinked at him and then said thoughtfully, "That's an interesting question."

The assistant said something in Korean to her, and Derrick felt a denseness to the sound of it, as if he was being deliberately excluded. He didn't like that, but he couldn't explain it, either, so he said nothing.

The shop girl replied in Korean that sounded like an affirmative, and then said to Derrick, "You can use Between in a lot of different ways—it's not about *can* you; it's about can *you*."

"Yeah, but what if I wanted to? What if I tried really hard? Could I?"

"Told you: it's not about *can* you, it's—"

"What if I could?"

"Then you'd probably be a lot safer from people trying to nab you out on the streets with tentacles."

Derrick nodded. "That's what I thought."

There was more to the world than he'd thought: that was fine. He just needed to come to grips with how to make it work for him —or, more importantly right now, how not to die. And as he stood in the shop with the shop girl and the assistant that he was beginning to believe might truly be a vampire, the floor felt as though it swayed under Derrick's feet, making him wonder exactly how long he would be able to hold onto that life.

"Flamin' heck!" the shop girl said, keeping to her feet without a problem and swaying with the movement. She sounded impressed. "Reckon they're trying to pull the whole shop out by the roots and take it back with them!"

The vampire said something in Korean that muttered and sulked, and Derrick asked, "Can they do that?"

The shop girl shrugged. "Probably not. Maybe. Reckon we'll see, before long!"

"I don't want to see before long!" Derrick protested. "I want to make sure they can't now!"

"Even if they do take it somewhere, they're not gunna be able to get in," the shop girl assured him. "It'll be a pain to put the shop back, but we've done it before. Hang on a tick, gunna check something."

"You've done it *before?*" Derrick blurted out, before he could stop himself, but she was already gone, leaving him to the narrowed eyes of the vampire assistant.

He didn't much like that state of affairs, but he couldn't say that whatever the shop girl had gone to check was ineffective, because a few minutes after Derrick began to find the assistant's gaze distinctly worrisome, the shaking beneath their feet ceased.

The assistant made a *hmf* sort of sound that seemed to signify both approval and confidence borne out, and grinned a lazy grin. Derrick wasn't sure the confidence was warranted, since the door and windows were still blocked out by the same inky blackness as it had been earlier.

Still, the shop girl was grinning a bit when she got back, and he did take that as a good sign. She had looked rather grim when the floor began to shake, and since she was the one most forthcoming with information, Derrick had insensibly begun to feel as though she knew the most.

"All done!" she said cheerfully to the vampire assistant. "Now, we wait!"

"How long?" asked Derrick, licking his lips. There was no time too long to wait to make sure that he wasn't dragged off goodness-knew-where by giant tentacles, but he had recently acquired a new pet and he didn't like to think of that pet alone and uncared for, getting up to mischief.

He was unsurprised when the shop girl said, "As long as it takes. In the meantime, why don't we try to figure out what that pair wants with you. I think—flamin' heck! That's all we need!"

Derrick, his eyes drawn irresistibly to the small point of moving black in the blackened glass door, saw to his horror that something wriggly and leggy and *hairy* was beginning to worm its way through. There was, in fact, a giant spider tortuously squirming its way out of the deeper black of the glass.

Derrick wasn't sure if it was sheer horror emanating from the door that seemed to seize his chest in a vice-like grip, or if it was something else entirely. As he pulled mechanically at the collar of his shirt, the shop girl and the vampire assistant exchanged a look.

"Ah!" said the vampire, his voice thick with irritation. "That is *too strong*! Now there will be a mess!"

"Look," said the shop girl, her grey eyes dwelling seriously on Derrick. "These two are going to a lot of trouble to make sure they get you. Anything you can think of that would set them after you?"

"I dunno—I work with kids?" Derrick found that he was sweating and stopped trying to pull at his collar in order to wipe it away. The horror was fading—was the shop girl responsible for that, or was it just the fact that the spider was still struggling to get out? "Maybe one of them is more important than I realised? I never really know about their families; it's a completely different context and I don't really have much contact with the parents."

"What do you mean, you work with kids?"

Derrick shrugged. He had learned that it wasn't wise to talk about his work, obliquely or otherwise, and he was uncomfortable with the idea of it more than ever now. He was safe enough in the shop for now, but he didn't know how safe the shop girl and the assistant were. If push came to shove, he was quite sure he could manage the shop girl, but the assistant had a snarling, dangerous look to him that Derrick was wary of, even if he wasn't a vampire.

He said, "I just...I move kids around. Get them from one place to the other without people seeing."

The shop girl's head tilted. "You're an extractor? Private?"

"Pretty much, yeah. Mostly I get money from the parents, so I suppose you can call that private. I'm on my own, if that's what you mean."

The last few words faltered away, because Derrick was too busy watching the giant spider separate itself from the bulging, beating softness of black it had emerged from. It should have plopped onto the ground with a soft, fat sort of a noise; instead, it clung to the wall, and at its hairy feet came another spider—and another, and another.

"Flamin' heck," said the shop girl. "What a rort—reckon we're gunna have to move the store again."

"I do not like this," the assistant said, with very sharp teeth.

"I don't flamin' like it, either!" she retorted. To Derrick, she said, "Not to worry; things'll just be a bit nasty for a while. I don't know if the spiders are real or not yet—don't know if they're venomous, either."

"They *look* real!!" Derrick said, the sweat rolling down his temple. He couldn't help the way his feet backed away from the door, or the way that his eyes were fixed on that one spider still crawling its way inevitably toward the floor.

He was aware, in a distant, horrified sort of a way, that there was another spot of black forming somewhere in his periphery—perhaps the far wall of the shop, to his left—but all of his attention was taken up with that door.

That door which, seething with a maelstrom of spiders that fairly churned a hole of blackness through the door, began to grow soft. Derrick, his heart sinking in very real terror, saw the bulging at the centre of it that looked like a spider roughly the shape of a soccer ball was about to come through, and gasped, "There's a bigger one coming!"

"Nope," said the shop girl, as the bulge resolved itself into a firmer shape that seemed to be layered over something very similar to a nose and a mulish chin. "Nope; reckon that's the bounty hunter."

"It's the—it's—*how?*"

"Dunno," said the shop girl. "Been trying to figure out how he's doing that for the last few minutes. Never seen someone interact with Between like this. If he was doing it directly, I'd be able to stop it."

The vampire said something that sounded very surprised but didn't make sense to Derrick.

Thoughtfully, the shop girl added, "It's like he's in a nightmare and the nightmare is what's coming through. Maybe he lucid dreams —well, lucid nightmares, anyway."

"I don't care what it is—stop it!"

"Can't," she said. "We'll just have to wait until it comes through and stop it then. I need to know how far the spiders are gunna come."

"I don't care how far the spiders come!" Derrick said in despair. He did: he cared desperately. But he cared more about the fact that the bounty hunter's head was now fully through the door, still straining and bulging forward. The thick slick of whatever inkiness covered the door and produced the spiders cleared slowly from his face, freeing his eyes and then his nose, then moving down inexorably toward his mouth.

"Flamin' heck!" said the shop girl, and now she sounded impressed. "Reckon that'd be hard to do."

"Kill him!" yelled Derrick, nearly beside himself at her tone and certain that things were about to get very bad for him as soon as that black receded further. "Kill him before he gets through!"

"Can't," said the shop girl. "He's only halfway through. That's not fair."

"He tried to kill me!"

"Did not," said the bounty hunter, his mouth emerging. He didn't look as if he was enjoying the spiders much, but he was still pushing through with a mulish sort of determination that churned Derrick's stomach more than the spiders did.

"I reckon I'm gunna have to wrap you up in a bit of Between when you get through," the shop girl said to him. The apologetic tone to her voice irritated Derrick a great deal.

The bounty hunter wriggled more vigorously. "You can't; I have to take that bloke in."

"No, I can," the shop girl said. "You prob'ly mean you don't want me to."

"Oh," said the bounty hunter. "I suppose that's true. Anyway, don't go covering me with Between—it'll turn into something nasty and that won't be fun for anyone."

"Look," said the shop girl. "I get that you're not used to talking to people—"

"Don't meet many people—mostly it's just the tentacles and spiders and stuff."

"Yeah; I get that. But if you want me to do anything you say, you've got to explain stuff. I can't just do what you tell me to do if I don't know why you want me to do it. I might not, even then; but at least I'll know if I should."

"Oh, right," the bounty hunter said. "I'm used to Behindkind just trying to kill me, not talk with me. He's a murderer, by the way."

The shop girl's eyes flicked thoughtfully toward Derrick, who yelled, "It's a lie! I've never done anything to this weirdo in my life!"

"He didn't do it to me, he did it to the kid whose photo is in my pocket," said the bounty hunter, still wriggling as though he couldn't help it. He was free fully to the shoulders now. "And about ten other kids until now. Check my breast pocket."

The shop girl did so, cautiously, and pulled out a glossy photograph, faceup. Derrick recognised the face straight away: it was the same one he had seen on tv a couple of weeks ago. It was also the one he had seen last week, when he threw dirt over it in a grave that he had made in a small garden hidden between three houses.

The shop girl didn't get a chance to look at it properly before spiders cascaded through the wall opposite them, two tentacles cascading with them, roiling and turning and churning and slicking right around Derrick without hesitation. He yelled—maybe he screamed—and struggled, but it was no use. The tentacles had him wholly, and they squeezed just enough around his chest to suggest that he'd better stop struggling if he wanted to keep breathing.

The shop girl, as if she'd read his mind, said, "Reckon you'd better stop struggling for now."

"You said they couldn't get in!" he yelled.

"I mean, I didn't expect anyone to get in via spider," she said, shrugging.

She didn't look sincere, and it occurred to Derrick to wonder, for the first time, exactly what the shop girl had been doing when she said she had to *check things* earlier. He squirmed in his moving, slick bonds, fingers clenched and oozing with the same viscous liquid that the tentacles were coated in.

At the door, the bounty hunter collapsed onto the floor in a wet, spidery plop that turned into thick ink on the floor, and rolled away from the mess. Derrick expected him to lunge across the floor at the end of that roll, knives out; instead, he stood, turned back to the door, and thrust his arm through the shifting blackness.

Derrick wasn't the only one who had thought he might attack: the shop girl watched his movements with a kind of amused surprise, while Derrick used the time to struggle as furiously as he could without drawing attention to himself. If the bounty hunter was stupid enough to waste time in bringing his secretary into the room along with him, Derrick would make good use of the time.

His own brain was moving too quickly to settle. How had they figured out he'd taken the latest kid already? He'd only taken her last night—he hadn't even had a chance to play with her yet. He saw the moment that the shop girl began to trust that the bounty hunter wouldn't suddenly dart across the room, and looked down at the photo in her hand instead.

"That's one of them," said the bounty hunter over his shoulder, as she scanned the photo. "Someone who didn't like the idea of her vanishing contacted us while we were already looking for this derelict. We've been looking for him all week."

"He's behindkind?"

"Nope. Human." He gave a huge tug and the secretary emerged from the blackness, fully to the waist, her eyes squeezed shut. She gasped a little and opened her eyes as the ink cleared from her face, but didn't look anywhere but at the bounty hunter. Derrick had the impression that she was trying to avoid looking at the spiders. "You told me that."

"Yeah, I know, but—"

"Why are we hunting a human killer?"

"Yeah," she said. "That. I'm pretty sure your speciality is in Behindkind. You've got the look."

The bounty hunter fixed his unsettling eyes on her. "I do? There's a look?"

"Yeah." The shop girl's eyes narrowed a little. "Is your secretary human?"

The secretary said, "Yes," as the bounty hunter assured the shop girl, "Oh yes."

"Good," she said. "I reckon you're going to need her."

"She's very useful," he said. "She does the connection thing. I just hunt the killers."

"You can't prove I did anything," Derrick said sulkily, ceasing his struggles now that he was noticed again. It wasn't an admission, but the shop girl's face closed as if she had taken it as one. He didn't like people being allowed to accuse him of things. "You won't find my DNA anywhere near the scene, and you won't find anything at my house, either."

"We already got the kid you've been keeping at the school," the secretary said. Her eyes, he had noticed, were usually a warm sort of brown: right now, they were as cold as ice.

"Also, we don't care about evidence and proving things!" said the bounty hunter happily. "The people who hired us don't care, either."

The shop girl shrugged at Derrick. "Looks like they don't care. D'you care, Jin Yeong?"

The vampire said "No," in Korean, but somehow something said the English version of it in Derrick's head.

Derrick clenched his teeth. Through them, he said, "You'd better let me go now, or you'll regret it. I don't go after kids because I can't take down a man—they're just more fun."

"I think we should kill him," said the vampire coldly.

"Not while he's tied up," the shop girl and the secretary said together. The shop girl added, "He's disgusting, but we're not murderers."

The bounty hunter opened his mouth as if to object, but the secretary found solid ground with one foot and then elbowed him swiftly and sharply.

"Anyway," said the shop girl, "we're not scared of murderers around here, so you can stop trying to frighten us. I've bitten bigger blokes than you."

Derrick glared at her. "If you knew who I was from the first minute, why play the games?" He was fond of games, but exclusively on his own terms—it was no fun if someone else set the rules.

"I didn't know who you were," said the shop girl. "I just knew you were flamin' bad news."

"You can't have," Derrick said in annoyance. "I'm *very good* at being a normal person!"

"Interesting thing," the shop girl said seriously, squatting down to speak face-to-face with Derrick over the soft but distinctly unpliable tentacles. "When someone mentions that their parents were killed by something otherworldly, it usually makes people ask questions. At the least, most people say *sorry*, or kinda freeze."

"I don't care about your parents," Derrick said bitterly. He was well and truly caught, but there was still time to think of a way to get out if he could only have some peace and quiet in which to think.

"Exactly," she said. "You didn't even blink: you just went on to asking the question that you were most interested in. It didn't even occur to you that you should be sorry about someone's parents being dead. That reaction isn't something you can hide—you probably don't even know you're doing it, because you haven't got the right brain connections to realise it's something you shouldn't do."

"You didn't trust me from the start," he said obstinately. He hadn't had a fair go. She'd been determined from the start to turn him over, and he resented that. He was *good* at looking normal—he was *good* at blending in.

"I mean, the first thing you did was to try and bully me into helping you," the shop girl pointed out. "I've got a nose for people who need help. But I was only sure when you started asking questions about how to use all the stuff you were finding out."

"He's good at blending in," said the bounty hunter. The compliment was dust and ashes coming from him. "That's why I was sent to find him. I'm good at finding things that look human and aren't quite."

"I'm human!" Derrick said, more incensed at that than anything that had preceded it. "That—*vampire* bit me! You know I'm human!"

"You're missing a few important parts," said the bounty hunter. "You're not behindkind, but I don't think you count as human, either."

"Yeah, that's the feeling I got," said the shop girl. "Some humans are less human than a few of the Behindkind I've met."

"I'm human," said the bounty hunter to her; then, as though he'd thought about it and something wasn't quite right, he added, "I don't count, though. We're glad you're not dead: we thought you must be friends, or that you'd be dead by the time we got in. Didn't think we'd get inside in time, but it looks like you two know what you're doing."

"You too," said the shop girl, pointing at the tentacles that wrapped around Derrick. "Good timing, that: I was just gunna kill him if he tried to hurt us."

"Money gets paid whether he's alive or dead."

"We don't just kill people," said the secretary, but she didn't say it as if it was a fact. She said it almost admonishingly, as if she was reminding the bounty hunter.

"Yes! Right!" he said. "We don't just kill people as our default. Not everyone is trying to kill us."

"Not everyone," said the shop girl. "But a fair flamin' lot of 'em are."

The bounty hunter's eyes lit up. "That's what I told Viv! She says everyone's experiences are different."

The secretary sighed, and that small sound seemed to draw the bounty hunter's attention to the fact that her foot was still stuck in the door. He spun around once again and made a dart to grab her beneath the arms, hauling until she squeaked and popped free of the door.

Her face redder than it had been, the secretary said in something of a pant, "You can put me down, Luca! I'm inside!"

Now that she was inside, the short, brown curls that had been pulled back on either side by combs showed themselves to be a deep russet instead of brown; her rimless glasses were round and very nearly invisible, and her chocolate high-waisted trousers were dotted with moisture that shone very slightly as though she had been touched by the same tentacles that now curled around Derrick. Together, she and the bounty hunter looked as though they'd stepped from the cover of a magazine from the '40s.

The bounty hunter said, "Sorry about the tentacles—it was the only way we could think of to get in here before he did anything to you both."

"It's a flamin' good reach," the shop girl said, her face impressed. "They're bigger than I thought they would be. Do they travel Between, or are they just reaching through? Are they disembodied?"

The bounty hunter's eyes lit up with the same unsettling, pupil-dilating interest that Derrick had seen earlier. That was a familiar look to him, too; he had caught it on his own face enough time in reflections to understand what it was. Excitement—interest.

"Not disembodied. She can travel Between, but only when it comes to water Between. She reaches when she needs to."

The shop girl asked, with interest, "You got a pet giant squid?"

"Giant octopus!" said the bounty hunter happily. "Meet Seffy!"

Two more enormous arms curled into the shop, wet and dripping copiously, the smell of salt water bleeding into the air with them. The shop girl patted those tentacles in fascination, gently and fearlessly; the vampire reared back, baring his teeth.

"Technically speaking, she can travel directly through Between without needing water," added the bounty hunter. "But the thing is that it's not comfortable for her. She prefers water."

The shop girl, her eyes alight, said, "I *need one.* What about magic? Can she use magic?"

The vampire made a sound of irritation and said to the secretary, "Now they will talk *forever.*"

"Oh well," said the secretary. She had a tired sort of a voice, like she was used to dealing with the bounty-hunter. "We might as well introduce ourselves somewhere a bit more...private."

She tilted her head slightly toward Derrick as she spoke, which sparked a surge of mingled panic and indignation in him.

"You can't leave me here!" he protested. He was more important than that—they couldn't risk losing him. And in the light of new information, he wasn't entirely sure that he wouldn't be lost in the maw of a giant octopus before he could get free and lose himself in the streets of Hobart again. "That thing will eat me!"

The vampire sniffed. "I have eaten this one. Why should you be frightened of it?"

"It's true," the shop girl said. "They sell 'em along the street in Busan, all bundled up. Not as big as Seffy, though."

"Seffy won't eat you," said the bounty-hunter. "She's strictly retrieval. You just won't like it if she retrieves you and takes you back to where she lives—there's not much air there."

"You won't get your money for me if I'm DOA," Derrick said, wriggling vigorously. "I'm too important for you to let me die."

The bounty-hunter's slightly manic grin made him shiver. "I don't get paid, anyway. And if it comes to people being important— you've only killed about ten people. I've killed at least a hundred."

A small line formed between the secretary's brow as her eyes shuttered briefly. "We should probably get back," she said. "We've already been away longer than we were meant to be. I've got to account for the time we spend away."

"Coffee, first," the shop girl firmly. "I wanna know more about the giant octopus."

"They are good to *eat*," said the vampire just as firmly, as he followed her past the counter and down the hall toward the back of the shop.

The bounty-hunter clapped his hands together, swivelling to face the secretary. "They said coffee," he said, pointing with his joined hands. "We can't not get coffee."

"*Luca*—"

But the bounty-hunter was already swivelling back around and had set off down the hall, leaving the secretary alone with Derrick and the tentacles of the otherwise absent Seffy. Derrick saw the line between her brows grow deeper, her lips pressing together. Whoever she was, the secretary wasn't a killer like the bounty-hunter—and she wasn't too happy about the bounty-hunter *being* a killer.

It was eating away at her, and Derrick knew exactly what to do with that. He said, softly vicious, "He'll kill you one day, too."

He saw her nostrils flare, but all she said was, "I don't take advice from kid-killers," and followed the others. Derrick heard her footsteps fading along the hall like the last beacon of hope and felt the air chill at least five degrees to the sinister slithering of tentacles.

Something touched his boot, cautiously, curiously, and he shivered, hunching into his bindings. Those bindings moved with him but never loosened, too responsive to be anything from the world that Derrick had thought he lived in until today, and he knew that there was no use trying to get out of them. It wasn't like he was going to get away. Not today. Today, he was simply going to try to survive. There would be time later to work out this new world into which he'd stumbled—and when he did, he would also figure out exactly how to use it to his own advantage.

And when he did that, not only the bounty-hunter and the secretary would feel his rage—the shop girl and the vampire would regret what they'd done to him today.

PINS AND NEEDLES

(Nothing to say here. You know the score: uncharted territory)

THERE WERE ALWAYS PINS TO FIND IN THE SHOP. MARLI CRAWLED about on the carpet most days to collect them, her eyes ranging to catch the silver glint that meant she had another one; she carefully poked each pin through her sleeve until she had a whole row of them, then trotted away to find a pincushion or a person willing to receive them. In Marli's experience, pincushions were more willing but rather less amusing recipients of her pins, especially if she chose to present the pins in the same enthusiastic fashion, point forward.

Someone, at some stage, must have been far too grateful—or encouraging—when Marli found the first pin, and it had become a habit for her to find them even after the reactions ceased to be as exciting.

Mum and dad were usually busy around the shop floor at this time of day, but today they were in the sneaky little sunroom at the back of the house that felt different to the rest of the shop. Marli enjoyed being in there too, but lately she had nearly gotten lost behind the couch, and something had tried to sneak her out the window when it opened more than it should have. She had been less frightened than annoyed, but mum and dad had started keeping the door closed after that, and today there was a guest in there as well.

Guests, Marli knew, were to be left alone unless introduced; in the meantime, there were pins to be found. The pin collecting might not have been so interesting—and might not have kept Marli entertained for as long as it did—if it wasn't for the friend who was visiting for the day.

There were a lot of friends who visited the shop, and some of them, like the knitting lady, who was here today, came back regularly. Sometimes there was the very short man who sounded angry but always pushed biscuits into her hand and counted pins with her in ways that she didn't understand, and who seemed to make her pins multiply in ways that weren't quite normal. There was a man in a wheelchair with hair that smelt of salt and brine when Marli climbed into his lap to put ribbon flowers in his brown curls, and there were always the tumble of boys that were really dogs when they wanted to be, and who never minded if she pulled their hair a bit too much when they played together.

The knitting lady was the one who had visited today, however. She sat in the chair in the corner, and knitted with wool and shadows while the shop moved around her; as her needles clicked, the aisles toward the back of the small store grew lighter. Marli wasn't old enough to know as much, but there were significantly more of those back aisles than the outward size of the store would suggest.

Marli took no notice of such things—she simply sat on the carpet and picked up pins, and when there were no more to be found she crawled or bunny-hopped or rolled over to another section.

When her sleeves were both full, she put one pin in the hem of her frock, promptly kneeled on it, and yelled angrily. Then she got up and went to sit next to the knitting lady's cool, peaceful silence and let her rage drift away while she pulled pin after pin out of her sleeves.

There was no pincushion there, but that was all right. Pins were very nearly needles, and even though needles were tiny silver things very much like pins, they were also very big wooden or metal things that the knitting lady knitted with.

So Marli removed pin after pin, running her tiny fingers along the length of them, and convinced each of them that they were really a needle. She convinced them so well that she soon had a pile of knitting needles beside her on the carpet. She had gotten through an entire sleeve's worth when the knitting lady, looking around in some confusion, at last settled her eyes on the pile.

"No more pins," said the old woman firmly.

Marli stuck out her lower lip very slightly, and then sniffed.

"No needles, either," the old woman said, before Marli could change another of the pins.

She sniffed again, and lifted her nose. The wolf boys always liked it when she made things be different.

"Look at you with your little nose," the old woman said, touching it with the end of one knitting needle.

Marli could have said, "*Ha*," and relieved her feelings, but she felt the air in the room shift as the rest of the shop connected with the sunroom. Instead, she said, "The door is opened."

"So it is," agreed the knitting lady. "Along you go, dear. I dare say they want you."

Marli huffed and climbed carefully to her feet, then padded on down the hall and toward the sunroom. The door was open, and she didn't doubt that she was welcome; everywhere in the shop that was open was hers to explore, and since it seemed that the more doors were closed, the more other things were somehow available to her, Marli had never felt trapped. It was pleasing to have one of those closed doors open, however.

She found a grey-suited man sitting in her favourite chair—a wooden-framed, leather-bound single-seater that wasn't always as independent of the carpet as it pretended to be. Marli stood by the door, watching the man, for a very long time. He let her watch without doing more than letting his eyes rest on her for a few moments and then glancing away again to look out of the window.

There were certainly a lot of shadows around him, and many of them were bloody, but the knitting lady had a lot of shadows around her, too. Marli knew, in a vague way, that these shadows were a part of the grey man rather than something moulded by him into another form, unlike the knitting lady's shadows; but she also knew that shadows weren't always bad.

Shadows only meant that there was something there to cast them.

Her mind made up, Marli stepped into the sunroom and skipped through the warm sunlight to shadows on the other side, and climbed into the grey man's lap, clinging to grey wool to scramble up.

"Good heavens," said the man, though Marli wasn't sure who he was talking to. "Should she be doing that, do you think?"

"This is *my* chair," Marli told him reprovingly, bracing her feet against wool-clad legs and gripping his lapels to balance herself well enough to look right into the grey eyes that were shadowed, too.

"It's her chair," said mum, from the doorway. She carried a tea tray into the room, balanced on her one hand with her body tilted just a little to support the weight from her missing arm. Marli smelt the familiar scent of coffee, and something else that was soft and flowery.

"How delightfully familiar," the grey man said, with a pained look down at his lapels, which were still clutched in Marli's small hands.

She knew what that look meant, so she threw her arms around the grey man's neck instead, giggling at the shadows behind him and stretching out a hand to that glittering miasma.

"Good heavens!" said the soft grey voice again. "I see this one takes after her mother."

He didn't, Marli noticed, hug her back. She said disapprovingly, "*Hug* me."

"I do apologise," said the grey man, and enfolded her in a brief embrace that was as gentle as it was subtly scented.

Marli chuckled happily and turned her cheek into the woollen shoulder and found something cold and golden touching her nose. She knew that she was too old to be putting everything into her mouth but despite that, she still couldn't help briefly closing her teeth on the enamel pin that was temptingly near on the man's lapel, delicious in its colour and shape.

A slim, dark hand reached past her and removed it from her mouth, exposing an inch of wrist from a silk suit-sleeve. This was the fun wrist. Marli gave a gleeful chuckle and gnashed her teeth at it as quickly as she could, surprising a laugh from the grey man, who let her go.

At once, the owner of the wrist crouched down, eyes narrowed, and twitched a finger at her. "You. No bite."

Marli waved a finger back at him and said, "No bite."

She was aware that although blood smelt delightful, it was murky and uninspiring once in her mouth. She still hadn't got over the point of biting things to test it out just one more time, but she was also old enough to know that the only safe person she could do so with was dad.

Accordingly, she waited until dad turned and sauntered across the room toward mum and the tea-tray; then she launched herself from the grey man's lap and caught dad around the shoulders, sinking her teeth into his neck.

If Marli had known what it was to be otherwise, she might have known that both her leap and her bite were beyond the expected capabilities of the average four-year-old. Since she didn't, her leap startled only the grey man, who said, "Good heavens!" once more as dad yelped and waved his arms and spun in a circle.

Mum simply moved the tea tray onto another table and sat down with her coffee while Marli clung to dad's shoulder, her teeth deep in flesh that throbbed with a heartbeat that was far too fast. In the early days of this play, Marli had been thrown off and caught gently more times than she had held on, but she was much stronger now.

She waited until dad stopped thrashing and dropped to the floor, then counted to three twice and released him. She flopped back on the floor next to him, giggling, and Dad turned his head to settle dark eyes on her.

He said, "Bad child," but Marli could see both sharp incisors in his grin and knew that he was proud of her.

"Should—should he be teaching her that?" enquired the grey man, as if fascinated.

"You're one to talk," said mum, but her voice wasn't angry. "I don't reckon it's a bad thing, though. It's a good idea to know when something really is dead, even if she's not going to be doing the deed herself."

"How short-sighted of me."

"Was it?" asked mum. "I figured it was concern. Looks like you've gotten a bit more open since I saw you last. You gunna let your friend come in and sit down, by the way? Or is she supposed to hang around and wait for you the whole time?"

Marli sat up in excitement as the room behind the grey man shifted, glittered a little more, and opened. There was a person-ness to the mass of shadows now—something that Marli had never yet seen.

"It seems as though she'd like to join us," the man said. "How delightful. But since you've already set out an extra cup, I rather suspect you knew she would."

Sitting up and straightening his suit-coat, dad said, "Of course she will want to meet us."

"Oh, I fancy you've met before," the grey man said, as a single foot stepped through the open air and touched down lightly on the sun-warmed floorboards. "But perhaps it's time for proper introductions: it really is time that you met my wife."

"Flamin' heck!" said mum. "You've been busy!"

"Lies," said dad. "Who would marry you, old man?"

Marli knew nothing about marriage and very little about introductions apart from the prohibition of biting people she had just met. What she did know about was the way her world moved and waxed and waned, and she delighted in the way that the room grew warmer with the addition of a second foot from the shadows behind the grey man—and the way that warmth seemed to touch him as well.

She climbed back into his lap, reaching a hand behind him, and found it caught in a much larger hand. That hand pulled back with some strength, as if it meant to pull her into the shadows with it, and Marli lost ground, falling against the grey man's lapel. Used to challenges from dad, she squeaked and resisted, her sharp knees digging into a chest that seemed impervious to them.

Aware of the reassuring hands that had closed around her ankles to steady and anchor her, Marli took a breath and reached out her other hand to join the first. Then, as she had always done, she pulled until what she wanted was out of shifting space and shadow, and into reality.

ZERO RESPONSIBILITY

(For all you Zero fans out there. We all need our emotionally unavailable giant sword-wielder occasionally.
And yes. It is out of order. Because apparently that's how things work around here...)

SHARPENING BLADES WAS ALWAYS SOOTHING. THE STEADY, repetitive actions; the certainty that the amount of effort and skill put into the job would produce exactly the desired result; the knowledge that one was preparing for one's own survival at a later stage—all were reasons that made up the total sum of the fact that in times of stress, sharpening blades was soothing.

That being the case, Lord Sero, once known as Zero—and still known, for the most part, to his friends as Zero—newly elevated to his position as *the* Lord Sero following his father's death, was once again sharpening blades.

His own personal blades were already as sharp as it was good for them to be, so Zero had moved on to the armoury, startling the old fae who ran the place and who swung old, stiff hips out of one of the rows of weapons and approached him at the first sign of incursion of his demesne.

"It's good to see you again, sir, if I may say so," he said, bowing as low as his hips allowed him to do, and extending that bow by one hand that had been gnarled by too many years grasping a hilt.

"Leonard," said Zero, recollection coming to him just a little too late to speak the name in decent time. There were a great many of his childhood days and hours that existed only behind the veil of a vaguely remembered awfulness that was bloody around the edges. "It's been a while."

"Indeed, sir," Old Leonard said. "I remember you and the Steward that was, hiding in here—that is, I remember him dragging you in and telling you to sit here or there. Barely anything of him there was, those days—just a stick of a thing with too many sharp edges. Oh aye, and you were an obedient child back then."

Zero's brows twitched themselves up of their own accord. There had been a very faint emphasis on the words *back then*, he was certain. "I'm not now?"

The mention of the person called *the steward* tickled with sharp fingers at the feeling that had brought him here to the armoury in the first place, and he was feeling pricked in more ways than one.

"I've always thought it was a pity for any of Sero's children to be too obedient," the old fae said deliberately. "The old Sero, that is. It's good to see you forging your own path, so to speak, sir. What can I do for you?"

That question, Zero found it very hard to answer. While he meditated swiftly on how exactly to answer it, Old Leonard's face lit up.

"Ah, it'll be *that*, won't it?" he said, and swung away again on his stiff hips. "Just sit there, sir. I've got something you can work on."

Then he had vanished, only to return nearly twenty minutes later with a small, single-wheeled cart absolutely bristling with weaponry that should have been sharp but wasn't.

"We got our annual lot of fresh blood in," explained Old

Leonard. "Normally, I'd make 'em sharpen this lot themselves; I'll be able to shock them with the fact that their master did it himself instead, and they'll have to run laps. They'll hate it!"

Zero didn't smile at the dry, mischievous chuckle that accompanied the words, but it wasn't from any lack of amusement. He had trained himself very early against showing any sign of emotion that could be used against him, and that early training, as useful as it had been, had all but frozen the muscles he might otherwise have used, out of sheer habit.

He had had more practise at smiling—and amusement—lately than formerly, but it was still an effort to remember to use those muscles. By the time he had done so in this case, it was already too late: the armoury master had chuckled again to himself, as if unsurprised, and headed back down toward the back of the armoury without waiting for an answering smile.

So it was that Zero found himself sharpening practise blades in the armoury, alone with his thoughts and unsure if he really wanted to be alone with them. Insensibly, he fell into his usual routine, stroking outward toward the point of the blade with his small whetstone, slow and regular; and as he did so, it felt as though his thoughts somehow smoothed and stroked outward just a little as well.

But although they straightened out beneath the constant movement, they still continued.

He had thought that with the Pet safe from the worst of the dangers that beset her—having done away with the worst of those herself—he would have less to work his mind and concern him. He had been wrong, because the Pet was the Pet, and trouble found her. What was to be done about that? Especially when the latest of those problems was one she welcomed, and one with which he was wholly unequipped to assist?

Not as large in his mind but still present was the matter of his inheritance: Zero hadn't intended to take over his father's estate when his father died. To be fair, he also hadn't intended not to do so. Yet here he was, going over the old place and running through the old names and crests to refine the dreck from the gold, and the deadly from the protective. Cleaning up corridors that went to places children should never have to go alone in the daylight, let alone in the kind of darkness to which such halls tended; and removing the last, stinking remnants of his father's influence from the flowery galleries.

Did he intend to tidy it up and close off everything that had lingering memories from his childhood, until every dark hall was closed forever, and the place sank back into the earth from which it had sprung, or did he intend to continue to tidy the place up and make use of it, exorcising ghosts as they came?

As if he was preparing to live there. As if he was preparing it for his children.

No, not his children. There was Pet to consider, however. Perhaps it was she he had had in mind when he came back home and began to go through everything with a fine-tooth comb, removing darkness even if he wasn't sure how to bring light in. And somehow, the light had begun to come regardless. Perhaps it had been there all along, just waiting for the darkness to be taken away.

Zero, turning to the strop from the whetstone for some of the more delicate knives he had just put an edge to, and finishing up the edge on each of them, now wondered afresh about his motivations for doing what he had done.

Had he had the thought that the estate would be ready for Pet when everything went wrong and she had nowhere else to go? Pet had a habit of landing on her feet and doing her best no matter what, but Zero didn't like allowing things he loved to fall, whether or not they were inclined to land on their feet, and he would never have consented to her marriage if he'd been given a real choice in the matter.

It led to dangerous things. It led to a life further entrenched in the Between of the worlds that had already proved so dangerous for

Pet, and which had cost her an arm. It led to—it led to exactly the sort of problem that was currently occupying his mind the most.

Zero still hadn't resolved most of the questions that plagued him, though he had gotten so far as to allow them to subside into a simmering unease at the back of his mind, by the time he was halfway through his self-imposed task. If only Pet wouldn't get into the kind of situations that meant her family were constantly worried, it would be—

Breaking through that thought, a familiar voice—and yet another of the reasons for his furious sharpening of blades—said, "There you are, sir."

Zero looked over his shoulder with a peculiar prickling sensation that was somewhere between anticipation and worry, and saw Palomena, his first Lieutenant, standing there with all her usual tidiness and silence.

"I've been searching high and low for you, sir," she said.

She didn't look as though she'd been searching high and low. She looked as though she'd known exactly where to look for him first. She also didn't sound reproachful, which Zero would have expected if he'd really put her to that sort of trouble.

"I've been here for the last two hours at least," he said.

"I'm not sure the armoury has been...er, available to the denizens of the house for the last two hours, sir," she said.

That was understandable. Now that it was his estate, the entire place would begin to mould itself to his wishes and ways of life; sometimes that would involve obscuring his whereabouts from the other occupants of the manor, and sometimes it would involve making life more uncomfortable for everyone who wasn't him.

"You'll have to take it up with the house if you don't approve of it," Zero said, testing the edge of the latest blade with his thumb. "It's an ancestral home, and it's been like this for centuries."

"I've never approved of that sort of thing," Palomena said, unexpectedly. "Especially for certain people and certain estates."

Zero put his knife down deliberately, taking his time to do it, and let down his end of the strop before he turned his entire attention on her. "You mean particularly me," he said. "Why?"

"Look at it this way, sir," she said. "If your niece were to try the kind of things she does so successfully in her own house here, would they work?"

"I would have stopped it years ago if I could do this sort of thing anywhere else," Zero said flatly. "I would have had her confined to her room where she couldn't get into trouble."

"Yes, sir," said Palomena, in the way one says, *That's exactly what I meant.*

"You think it was better for her to have her arm taken off piece by piece? You think it's better that she married a vampire and is now—"

"I think," Palomena said smoothly, "that your niece took down an entire world order while also fighting you tooth and nail to make sure that she could do what she thought was right, even if it cost her everything. I think her arm was her own to give, and not yours to keep. The kind of assistance that estates give to overbearing owners is exactly the reason that you left in your younger years, I believe."

Instead of answering that, Zero asked, "You think it encourages the heads of the family to exert control they shouldn't exert?"

"Of course it does. Why try to convince your progeny of anything when you can control and frighten them into doing what you want them to do instead? When they're aware that every part of their life is surrounded by and controlled by you, they either fall into line or into danger. A well-run estate is a weapon on the inside as much as it's a weapon on the outside."

Zero, who knew the truth of this experientially, but who was stubborn enough to think that if he had the running of things, he would run them differently—more kindly, thanks to what he had learned while dealing with his niece, albeit with a sufficiently strong hand—persisted.

"You can't think that a good master running an estate is the same as a bad one."

"There's only a few years and a few disagreements between a good master and a bad master when it comes to an estate being run on the wishes and desires of a single person without regard to the rest of the household."

"You think power always corrupts, then?"

"If you're uncomfortable with that, say that it encourages selfishness," Palomena said. "After all, if you're the master of the house, you have the right to have everything running as you want it. And if anyone pushes back, you have the power to make life very uncomfortable for them, even when you're not doing it consciously—the whole system works for you without you having to think about it. And after a while, it's offensive when people don't acknowledge your power, so you make sure they have to. Then you're grasping for that acknowledgement over smaller and smaller things."

"It's not about controlling things," Zero said, picking up a blade at random. He found that he had already sharpened it and put it down with some bemusement. It never had been about controlling things. It had always been about keeping things safe. Particularly little soft things that didn't seem to be able to keep themselves safe. "It's about serving the denizens of the estate and having the power to keep them safe."

"If it was about service, estate owners would be happy to serve without it," Palomena said. "Instead of trying to insist on acknowledgement. Did you know that estates where everyone is given a share of the estate and place in it are known to—"

"Estates have to be run by one person if they aren't to fall apart," Zero said. He said it with a kind of finality that he unconsciously expected to put an end to the conversation with its authority.

"I think we'll have to agree to disagree on that," said Palomena, and there was a very large silence at the end of her sentence that Zero took far too long to fill with the thing that should have been in that space.

"You forgot to say *sir*," he said. He thought about it and added, "You've forgotten it for the last ten minutes, actually."

"My apologies, sir," she said.

Zero had a moment of deep disappointment. He wasn't sure what he had expected her to say, but it hadn't been that. He picked up the free end of the strop and began setting the final edge on another pre-sharpened blade, annoyed with himself for being surprised and disappointed, and still disappointed beneath that.

Clamping down on that disappointment and trying by sheer force of will to turn it into disinterest—and achieving a gloominess that was nevertheless close enough to serve as the same—Zero proffered his own apology. "I'm sorry to have made it hard for you to find me," he said.

That would give her a chance to say that *it was nothing*, or *not at all, sir*, and Zero found that he very much wanted to hear something of the kind from Palomena at this very moment.

Instead, she started that prickling feeling up again by asking unexpectedly, "Are you all right, sir?"

"Of course," he said—a stock reply to help hide the fact that he didn't know how to reply to enquiries of this sort. The blade, now motionless in his hand, felt awkward. "I'm always well."

"Yes, sir," said Palomena. "I suppose that's why you're working your way through the armoury, one blunt edge at a time."

Zero would have liked to have said, coldly, that he was working through the armoury because it had been kept in bad repair while he'd been gone, but Old Leonard was standing within earshot again and didn't deserve to be thrown to the wolves.

He also didn't put it past the old fellow to give him the sort of reproachful look he was least proof against—especially when Old Leonard must have been as well aware as Zero was, that he had done his lord a service.

Instead, he asked, "What do you want?"

"It's not so much what *I* want as what the Enforcers want," Palomena said, uncrushed.

She always was uncrushed, unlike the Pet, who had always been dampened by his cursory replies to tentative forays of—affection? Care?

Was Palomena being caring toward him?

Zero, insensibly, began to sharpen the blade again. "What do the Enforcers want?"

"There's a problem with one of the computers, sir, and someone told the higher ups that you've had experience with things like that."

"I beg your—computer? We have *computers*? I know nothing about them—I was sent via email once when we first met…a certain acquaintance—and I have no other experience with them."

That wasn't quite true, but the small amount of further experience he had had with computers hadn't given him any further knowledge of them.

"I daresay you don't, sir, but you absolutely know more than anyone else in the enforcers, and I've been sent to bring you along so that we can figure out exactly what's going on. They suspect that someone has put some sort of magic virus in it to spy on the command centre it's in."

"They'd be better off throwing it out," Zero said dourly. "I don't know what to do with it."

"Perhaps not, but they want you to look at it regardless."

"It'll only end in me throwing it out the window," he warned.

Palomena seemed indifferent to the idea of computers being thrown out windows. "I'm sure they'll trust your judgement, no matter what you do with it. I have a feeling that the older ones think of it as an eldritch abomination and the younger ones think of it as…well, they seem to think of it as an eldritch abomination as well, but they're a lot more excited about it. Why don't you consider it a useful distraction?"

"A distraction from what?" Zero asked, at last looking up again—daring her to answer.

"I'm sure you know best about that, sir."

He made an impatient movement, then thrust the nearly-ready blades back onto the bench in front of him and stood. "We might as well get it over with," he said. "Where is it?"

"It's the Cygnet office," Palomena said. More helpfully, she added, "It's the one where the town is all on the same street and there are five bakeries."

"Are the bakeries involved in the problem?"

"Not that I know of, sir."

Zero hazarded, "Are the patrons in danger?"

"No, sir," said Palomena. He wasn't sure if she was amused or confused.

He said suspiciously, "You said there were bakeries. I expected that it was pertinent information. Don't give me information that isn't pertinent."

"Yes, sir," said Palomena. "Only I thought that we might be able to get a few things on the way home, thus making it extremely pertinent. There's a Polish bakery that has several different kinds of pastry that are all *very good* and—"

Zero stared at her. "You want to stop for *pastries* on the way home?"

"It might make the trip out worthwhile, sir," she suggested.

ZERO WASN'T QUITE sure how it happened, but somehow or other, not even half an hour later, he was striding along the main—and only—street that made up the bulk of the town of Cygnet. The glimmer of Between still clung to his boots and flickered in the reflected strands of his hair as he passed windows; it also made small, moonlit gleams in Palomena's tightly braided hair in the flickering reflections. Too many of the buildings along the street were older, grand places with ties to older Tasmania, and the shifting Between world they had moved through—deeper and more dangerous than the human world that skimmed above them—had ties to those bricks and stones and beams.

"Bit sticky here, sir," Palomena said, brushing down the front of her uniform almost instinctively and stopping to scuff her boots slightly. "The office isn't far."

That was another reason for the way the other world still tried to cling: a Behindkind office sitting in an older street tended to draw all the Between threads toward itself and make a miasma of reality that was too fuzzy around the edges for safety.

At the centre of that fuzziness was a brick and wood building with maroon accents that looked as though it had been built in the 1920s; it was currently a restaurant, but Palomena ignored the open door in the vestibule that led toward a dining area, and went on toward the carpeted stairs instead.

Zero, following her, found himself treading over moss and flowers instead of carpet within a few steps, and felt a cool breeze that might have been air-conditioning if it hadn't been for the scent of hyacinths that floated along with it. At the landing, he stepped into a room that wasn't quite a room but wasn't quite *not* a room, either.

There were windows, and they did show a comprehensive view of the street when he looked out of them, but the walls didn't seem quite sure about being walls instead of hedges, and the carpeted floor hadn't yet made up its mind about being carpet or moss. The few desks that existed weren't as structured or canonically desk-like as they might have been.

"You can't come in here," said the pooch-bellied satyr at one of the desks. He leaned back in his chair despite the words, and Zero didn't get the impression that the satyr had any intention of trying to stop anyone coming in.

"We were sent by head office," Palomena told him. "They said you have a computer problem."

"It's no problem to me," the satyr said. "It sits over there and does its work, and I sit over here and do mine. If the lot of you stopped fussing around it and let it be, we'd all have a few less problems."

Palomena's eyes met Zero's briefly before she turned back to the satyr. "Someone said it was spying on the office?"

"What if it is? We don't do anything here. Let it spy."

Zero said briefly, "I'll take a look at it," and left Palomena with the satyr. He didn't want to be investigating a computer, but he wanted even less to be arguing with a satyr about whether or not anything done in a Behindkind office was worth spying on.

As he approached the computer, several heads popped up and around dividers, hedges, and the edges of desks that weren't quite where they ought to be.

"Finally!" someone muttered. "Maybe we can all get back to work again once it's fixed!"

Someone else said audibly, "*What* work? The only time I hear your little faun feet tip-tapping around is when the boss comes up here."

Zero focused on one of the faces—the small, round one that looked most serious—and said, "Come around here."

The head bowed briefly, then twitched back behind its hedge so that a small, furry centaur could trot into view, her horsey hindquarters as close-clipped and neat as her hair. Her sleeveless business shirt was tied neatly at the bottom in lieu of a belt.

He asked her briefly, "What's been happening?"

"We're losing chunks of the day," she said. "Ever since Between grew all over the computer cords and the flowers came out, we've been missing pieces of time—or running them all over again—and we're getting informational displays we shouldn't be able to access. It also seems to be sending information it shouldn't be sending."

"What sort of information?"

"Yesterday, it told head office that Doris has been taking two-hour lunches instead of one-hour lunches."

"It's not true!" called someone from behind a hedge. Doris, most likely.

"Is it sending anything more dangerous?"

"Not so far, no," the centaur said. "But it shouldn't be sending anything at all. It's not connected to the human internet, and our systems don't connect to human systems."

"Yes," said Zero, as if he understood what that meant. He did, vaguely. He said, "I'll take a look."

"It usually only repeats lunch hour," called out the satyr. "And that's the opposite of a problem."

Zero ignored that and stared at the computer as Palomena came to stand beside him.

The computer was...a computer. He gazed at it for some time, trying to remember everything he knew about computers. The thin, box-like piece at the top was the monitor, and displayed whatever was needed. The box below the desk was the brain to the machine. The cords that ran to and from both of those pieces were to be expected, but...

"Do you think there should be flowers growing from the power cord, sir?" asked Palomena.

Zero doubted it. He also didn't think there should be moss creeping along the top of the monitor, or fungi blooming between the keys of the keyboard, either. Despite each of those things, however, the screen of the computer was lit, the keyboard was also functional, and a steady, comfortable *whirrr* proceeded from the lower part of the machine.

In fact, that comfortable *whirrr* was very nearly a purr, and if Zero had found it wise to attribute living characteristics to a machine, he would have said that the machine was pleased—perhaps even smug.

As his eyes ranged over the machine, looking for anything and everything that could be considered out of the ordinary, that steady *whirrr* sped up and became eager, purposeful. Fungi puffed itself through the keyboard in its zest for life, and a sprinkling of blue-bells sprang up along the connecting cord from monitor to CPU.

"Do we think it should be doing *that*, then, sir?" asked Palomena, watching the blossoming of new life with a fascinated eye.

"Unplug it!" said a shrill voice that Zero recognised as the previously-mentioned Doris. "If I have to do the same work over again *once more*, I'm going to write a strongly-worded letter to head office!"

"It might be a good idea, sir," murmured Palomena, her eyes flicking over the swiftly spreading flora.

Zero, who could feel the movement of something deeper and more insidious deep in the moss beneath his feet, said, "Everybody out!"

Nobody needed to be told twice: everyone except the satyr variously cantered, ran, bowled, barged, and flew toward the door, then milled up against it like water as it resisted their every effort to leave the room.

Zero and Palomena, bringing up the rear, exchanged looks; Zero shouldered his way through the small but frantic crowd, and found that there was no longer an opening where there had once been one that led to the landing. Instead, a cobwebby something that was neither cobweb nor quite *something* wove away the reality that had been a door and made it blank, unapproachable, and unable to be passed through.

"Unplug it!" said the same shrill voice, and this time, Zero could see that the voice belonged to a grey, wizened creature that was probably a gargoyle. Doris, the aforementioned gargoyle, looked as though she could do with a few solid meals of stone to help with the wizened look, but there was nothing wavering about the scowl she had turned on him. "We should have unplugged it from the start and thrown it out the window! No good comes of meddling with human wares!"

Zero's eyes met Palomena's once again. One of his shoulders lifted slightly and he opened his mouth to say, "We might as well try it," when Palomena said, "I do hope you aren't going to say *I told you so*, sir."

He held her eyes just a moment longer, aware that there was amusement in his own. "We might as well try unplugging it, at least," he said.

"Wouldn't bother," the satyr said. He was the only one who

hadn't left his desk, and now one of his hooves rested on that desk as he flipped through a magazine. "It'll stop again when it's done."

"It hasn't locked the doors before," pointed out the miniature centaur. "Or closed us off from the restaurant."

"It doesn't matter what it does when we're in here; the thing is that it always stops again after a couple of hours."

"Excuse me if I don't find that particularly comforting!" said Doris indignantly. "I didn't agree to work in these conditions!"

"You didn't agree to have two-hour lunches, either, but—"

"It's a lie! I didn't have a two-hour lunch; that *human-made* abomination restarted time when I'd just finished my lunch break, and I had to eat it *all over again*!"

Zero left the bickering behind him at the door and strode back across the mossy carpet to the computer. He wrenched out the cord that connected the monitor to the lower box and picked it up with one hand, turning toward the window.

"Wrong bit," said the satyr, without looking up.

Zero would have liked to have ignored him, but found that he couldn't. He turned back and tore out the cord that linked the lower box to somewhere below the moss, hefted that up beside the monitor, then crossed the room at a swift clip, and hurled the entire lot —monitor, cords, lower box, moss, flowers, and fungi—through the window.

The whirr of the computer went into overdrive, humming through the room and through his teeth, and it occurred to Zero only a moment after defenestration that the same whirring had been continuous as he strode across the floor—not ceasing even when he pulled out all the cords that should have been powering the computer.

"Reset!" said a friendly, computerised voice above the all-consuming whirr of the computer.

The monitor sailed back through the window in reverse, trailing its cords and followed by the cpu, and tumbled through air heavy with sound and flowers until it settled back on its desk. The two power cords sank respectively through the mossy floor and back into the cpu, and the monitor's screen lit up once again.

"Goodness!" said Palomena, staring at it. "I really thought that would work!"

There might have been a very faint snuff of amusement from the satyr at the reception desk.

Zero, who had also thought his plan a solid, if not particularly nuanced one, asked the centaur grimly, "Is this what you mean when you said it re-runs time?"

"Well, we haven't tried to throw it out of the window before, but yes. It's never stopped us from leaving before."

"When did it first start happening?" asked Palomena. Her eyes scanned the text that scrolled across the computer screen, but she didn't read it as a human would have, and Zero had the impression that she scanned it without understanding.

"A few months ago," the centaur said. "It was Wednesday, I remember—we'd just got our weekly work packets through the portals, and suddenly there were two of everything. Then there was only one again, but the packets we had were copies. We never found where the originals went."

"Then," said Doris, her stony nose nearly quivering, "last week, the nasty thing started sending back messages about our activities from hour to hour. And the messages were *wrong*."

"We can't prove it was the computer," said the centaur. "It could have been *someone* having a joke."

The satyr, toward whom this very pointed remark was addressed, grinned and went back to his magazine. "I don't get paid enough to send an hour-by-hour report," he said. "They wouldn't read it even if I did send it. They just like collecting the reports."

"They think someone is reading them," Palomena said. "That's why we're here."

"Anyone willing to sit down and read an hour-by-hour report of what Doris is up to deserves what they get," the satyr said, turning a page. He picked up a silver clawed back-scratcher that was lying on the desk and applied it vigorously down the back of his shirt. "That sort of information isn't going to bring down the world Behind. It wouldn't even bring down the office, unless someone died of boredom while reading it and they classified it as friendly fire."

"I put itching powder on that," said Doris, with conversational malice.

He stared at her. "No, you didn't."

"You'll see," she said, the skin by her nose wrinkling in satisfaction. "Just wait. It sets in nice and slow."

The satyr's hoof dropped from the desk, and he sat up straighter. Zero got the impression that he was trying not to wriggle the shoulders he had just been scratching. He tried not to sigh in irritation: the entire situation was beginning to feel more and more familiar. He was not fond of working with messy people, and this office was very definitely a mess. He couldn't pinpoint anyone who was in charge, which was evidently where most of their problems were coming from, and all of the office-workers evidently disliked each other.

No leadership and no directions made for a sloppy office—or unit. No doubt that was how the computer was doing what it was doing. Though how the office had been one of the best performing offices over the last few months, he had no idea. That was something that had been included in the swift briefing he had received from Palomena on the way out to the office: this particular location had gone through several managers in the previous months, the first leaving just after the human computer was installed and citing discomfort with human-made items being incorporated into a Behind office, and none of the others had stayed much longer than a week or two.

Zero didn't particularly blame them: he would find the sheer insubordination and level of bickering difficult to deal with—but he would have dealt with it instead of leaving.

Of the miniature centaur, who seemed to be the most sensible of the lot, he asked, "Have they sent anyone else to look at the computer?"

"Every time they try sending in a new boss or one of the bosses comes down to look us over, whoever they send has a quick look at it. They go away pretty quickly, though."

"How often is that?"

It was the satyr who answered, one shoulder very slightly higher than the other with his efforts not to wriggle. "We haven't had a manager since the last one quit a month ago, so the bosses come in to check on us every week."

The miniature centaur giggled nervously. "I don't think the computer likes upper management," she said. "It always seems to get worse when they visit."

"If they'd let it be, we wouldn't have problems," the satyr said. "If we all minded our business, we could get our work done and go home at the end of the day like usual. It doesn't bother us when we don't bother it."

"It bothers me," Doris said, under her breath. "I don't like human things in decent office life, and I don't like eating two lunches."

Zero, annoyed at the plethora of useless information when he had asked a very simple question, ignored Doris and said, "It's obvious that the computer is affecting the entire office, so we'll try to separate it from the office. Once it has no hold, the door should return and the rest of the office should go back to normal. I'm surprised that none of the managers who came to look it over tried something of the kind."

"You want to try a containment field?" said Palomena, considering it. "There are enough of us, I should think."

The satyr went to pick up his back-scratcher, paused, and glared at Doris as he said, "I don't want to go meddling with the computer. The managers are always meddling with it, and it always turns out badly."

"I'm not asking you what you want to do," Zero said coldly. "I'm telling you what we're going to do in order to solve the problem."

"As far as we can tell, you're the one causing the problems," pointed out the satyr. "You're the one who threw it out the window. It's always let us out before."

Zero threw him a cold look. Being cheeked by a grown satyr shouldn't have been as annoying as being cheeked by his niece, who was younger and less worldly wise, but somehow it was. In fact, it was even more annoying. It could have had to do with the smirk the satyr wore. Pet didn't smirk.

He said to the gargoyle, "Doris, take the side opposite the window with the two willow-ladies; centaurs to the left of the room, and anyone biped over to the right. My lieutenant and I will take the window side."

Doris jumped to do as she was told, her stony wings making tiny, pebbly rattlings as she did so, but the centaur paused and said reluctantly, "I don't think that's the best idea, sir."

"It doesn't even make sense," the satyr said. He had also moved to do as he was told, but he did it in a desultory and strolling sort of way that suggested that Zero was lucky he was doing it. "Doris sits over behind *that* wall where her stony little heart can be crabby along with all the marble, and pony-tush parks her miniature behind over where the grass is longest so she can have a snack every few minutes."

"It doesn't matter where they normally sit," Zero said shortly. "We're not here to work. We're doing this to contain the computer for long enough to get you out of the office so that someone who knows what they're doing to come in and fix the computer."

"The computer doesn't need fixing when you lot don't come in here and try to meddle with it," pointed out the satyr.

"Be quiet and take your position!" snapped Zero. He saw the satyr open his mouth—no doubt to remark that he was *already* in his position—and asked the centaur with thin patience, "Are you ready?"

"In position, sir. But I really think we're just going to annoy it."

"It's a computer," Zero said, his patience even thinner. "It doesn't have feelings. Start. *Now.*"

There was an instantaneous surge of magic from all sides of the room, converging on the computer and surrounding it in a square of glassy, moving power. It held for a good thirty seconds before it fluttered briefly, sucked in on itself from all sides, and drained away into the computer.

"Stop!" Zero said sharply, and there was a collective gasp of relief as each of the office workers let go of their stream of power and watched it disappear into the now even more shiny computer.

There was the staticky sound of processing, then the computer said, "Nom nom. Resetting time: two hours."

Everyone stared around at the others in consternation, and one of the willow-women gave vent to a small howl of irritation.

"Very nice," said the satyr. "Now we're in here for another two hours. Very successful, I call that."

"Take a break," Zero said to them all, ignoring the satyr. "We're going to need more strength for this. Eat something if you need to, and we'll try again in half an hour."

THEY TRIED AGAIN in half an hour. They also tried again in one hour's time, while Zero worked his hardest to stay even-voiced as he reminded the office workers that they needed to output at the same rate and with the same strength as their opposites, and they told him with some indignation that they were doing their *best*.

Then they tried again every half hour for the next two hours, to no more success than they had begun the first time. The computer, no matter what they did or how they did it, simply ate up the containment field and cheerfully announced to the room that time had restarted.

At length, wildly annoyed and at the very end of his patience, Zero told them with a great deal more sharpness than earlier that they could all take another rest.

"Some of you are getting tired more easily than the others," he added. "We'll join up again when everyone is rested."

He meant it as a barb, and it was obvious that they took it as such—a good few of them looked resentful, even if they did so behind cubicle dividers and with their faces turned away. Zero looked around for Palomena and found that she had, in the last effort, gone to help the weakest side of the room without informing him.

He was already irritated, so that irritated him more than it would have usually. Technically, he trusted Palomena to do what was best in almost every situation without his direct leadership: today, he was just raw enough from his interactions with the office workers —who by now, at least, had stopped answering back and trying to talk—to find it distinctly irritating.

It struck him with another pang of irritation as he walked toward her that Palomena was also looking somewhat annoyed; while she had every right to be annoyed, he didn't think she should be turning the look on him.

"Sir," she said, when he was close enough, "perhaps it would be a good idea to gather with the staff and talk about it with them instead of just telling them what to do. There seems to be some sort of conversation going on in murmurs around the place, and—"

"I don't have *time* to take every opinion into consideration!" Zero said as softly as he could, through his teeth. "I can't be in here all day. I'm expecting news any minute—with Pet in the condition she's in—"

"Then may I suggest," said Palomena in a likewise low voice that had some bite to it, "that you listen to the people who work in this office and who presumably know what they're talking about when it comes to the office they inhabit and the chattel they obviously have some experience with?"

There was that silence at the end of the words again—a silence of something missing, or maybe of something extra. It took Zero several seconds as he stared down at her, to realise that Palomena's left hand gripped his right arm just above the elbow. It wasn't a commanding or a soft grip: it was a grip that pinched him into the present and out of his frustration, and allowed him to think things over again with a clearer mind.

This was not his lieutenant Palomena. This was the Palomena who didn't call him sir and worried about him—him!—and who didn't hesitate to push back when she thought he was doing something he shouldn't be doing.

Come to think of it, it was this part of Palomena that made her a good lieutenant, too.

Zero drew in a deep breath, let it out, and clamped down very hard on his pride. Then he nodded and crossed the room toward the desk where all of the office-workers had almost insensibly gathered together, talking softly amongst themselves.

They watched him uneasily, but when he said to the miniature centaur, "What do you suggest we do instead of what we have been doing?"

"Well, sir—no, shut *up* Terrence!"

The satyr shut his mouth and this time twitched his shoulders without trying to hide that he was doing it.

"Well, sir," began the miniature centaur, "we've noticed that the computer runs with the least problems when we come in and do our work as usual without fuss and bother. It only seems to start getting involved when someone sets it off by being a bit too picky or micro-managing—it doesn't like time being wasted with extra...things."

"I see," said Zero, into the heavy silence that followed. "Were none of you going to mention this?"

"You were pretty set on what you thought needed to be done, sir," pointed out the centaur. "And in our experience, most managers don't like to be told to loosen up and let us get on with things because they're trained to...well, manage. They seem to forget that we were also trained to do what we do. The computer really doesn't seem to like fidgets and micro-managers."

"That's why it twits Doris so often," said the satyr. "Likes to play little tricks on her."

Doris muttered something about *human contraptions* again but said a little louder, "If everyone else is happy with it, far be it from me to make a fuss!"

"It does seem to like having a manager, though," added the centaur. "We were just talking about it now, and Terrence mentioned that it also seems to eat up the energy that we put out when we work—it just doesn't like the seasoning much when there are certain managers involved."

"I see," Zero said again. "Then it seems like I've made this day much more difficult for you."

"I mean, you were very useful, sir! Having you here really made it clear to me what works and what doesn't. We wouldn't have realised that it's eating the energy if you hadn't made us do all of that—or that it hates that kind of energy."

She was trying to make him feel better, and that made Zero's insides crawl with discomfort.

"Were any of you planning on telling me that, either?"

"We would have tried," the satyr said. "Eventually. Usually managers need a bit more time to soften before the computer lets up. You're the first one to stop mid-rant."

"I wasn't—" Zero bit his tongue on the defensive reply that he hadn't been ranting, and said instead, "What are you suggesting?"

"We think we ought to get on with our day's work," said one of the tree-women. "We're already behind because of what happened when you got here, so it'll probably take us a couple of hours."

"Very well," said Zero. "Then let us begin."

It was almost impressive to see how efficiently and unhesitatingly everyone returned to their seats and went about their work. If Zero really had been a manager, he probably would have been very pleased with what he saw. He might also have felt somewhat useless.

Since he did feel rather useless anyway, Zero joined Palomena in the centre of the room and leaned against the computer desk, studying the office as a steady hum of business and work began to rise around them, watching for the first signs of something useful.

There was power—huge power—that also rose in the air along with the sound of the office. To him, it was formless and useless, floating around the room in clouds that obscured the office-workers, who paid no attention to it, as if they were so used to it that it was just a part of life.

Zero began, "Am I—" and cut himself short. He wasn't sure what he was supposed to be doing. "Should I direct you to your tasks? This isn't really working."

"That's because you aren't doing your job, sir," the centaur said, peeking around the side of her cubicle. Several of the office-workers murmured their agreement, and Zero saw Palomena's dark eyes lighten with sudden understanding. He didn't have a similar understanding, so it was a relief when she added, "You're the one who has to gather it all up and feed it to the computer; it always processes through the manager, one way or another. I think that's why the computer is picky about managers."

"So I just...sit here and let it go through me. I'm not supposed to tell you what to do, and I'm not supposed to put my own power in?"

"You don't need to tell us what to do," Doris said, her leathery voice uncertain. Zero understood that uncertainty: Doris, at least, liked being told what to do, and found herself more comfortable when under instruction. Perhaps that was what made him listen to her. "We all know what we're supposed to be doing. We know how to do it, too. You'll get all your power from us; all you need to do is direct it into the right place."

He didn't miss the faintly anxious look that Palomena turned on him, and tried very hard not to let the irritation in his voice out when he said, "You don't need to look so worried; I'm listening. I don't need to put any power in; I just need to process yours into the computer."

"You're the interface," Palomena said. She turned to the centaur. "That's right, isn't it? He's a stand in for your usual manager, so he's the interface with the computer: he'll take in all of your energy as you expend it, and focus it into the computer to bring about an end-of-day scenario. Once you've all done your day's work and it's processed through him and the computer, the computer will have no reason to keep the door locked."

"That's what I think," the centaur confirmed. She exchanged a glance with the satyr and added, "That's what we think."

"It hasn't been transmitting the information it copies; it's been eating it," Zero said, in realisation.

"Told you," said the satyr to Doris. "Nobody would want to know about your two-hour lunches."

"It doesn't feel like much," Zero remarked. He could feel the power pushing up against him like slightly heavier smoke, and he took it all in, tempering each of the different strengths and kinds until it made a single strength and consistency.

He didn't like the idea of doing so little—of being so little in command, or supplying so little to the group effort when he was supposed to be there in the capacity of a helper.

"Trust me," said the centaur, as he put his hand on the computer to begin the transfer of power. "It's actually very exhausting. You're going to need all your strength just to take in all of our different work energies and churn them out again into a simple stream of information for the computer. The managers are always dead tired when they leave, and that's when they don't know what they're doing."

Zero thought that she was trying to make him feel better again, but as soon as the power he had transmuted left his hand and went into the computer, he felt the drain. The computer was ready and waiting, and it took in everything he had already prepared and sucked at his soul for more.

The outer world and the office grew dull and fuzzy around him as he concentrated on the myriad sources of power and converted them to a single stream of useable, edible power from the computer, which never seemed to be satisfied and never seemed to stop eating.

If he had not been who he was, Zero knew distantly that things might have been very different today. He had made things worse by throwing the computer out the window and then by throwing power at it willy-nilly, and had he not had access to the kind of energy and power that he had access to, he might have ended the day in a far worse condition than he finally ended it.

Even with his gifts and natural resilience, Zero was sweating and shaking slightly by the time the computer, in a friendly sort of voice, said, "Work day completed. Optimal output reached. Everyone has been awarded a gold star."

The office-workers cheered in a tired sort of a way, but the satyr snorted and headed for the door.

"Where are you going?" Zero asked him, wiping the sweat from his brow and taking a moment to collect himself before he straightened and pushed away from the desk.

Palomena, who had been slightly hovering, backed away when she saw him stand without staggering, and Zero felt vaguely that he would have preferred to have a hand on his arm again.

"Work day's finished," said the satyr, in reply. "I'm off."

And to Zero's utter astonishment, the door opened under the satyr's hand. The satyr grinned at him and said, "Told you so. This thing just doesn't much like micromanaging."

There was a very minor stampede for the door, headed by Doris the gargoyle, who huffed and puffed until she was through it and into the hallway. They milled about and down the stairs, until all of the Behindkind were on the street in various states of camouflage and dress, some of them still pulling on their jumpers and cardigans.

It wasn't quite evening, but there was a definite darkening to the afternoon around them. Zero, who wanted nothing more than to return to his own demesne and ask for the latest news of his niece, forced himself to see the job through to the end.

"None of you have to return to the office until something is done about the computer," he said to them, drawing in a deep breath, and with it, energy. "Mention my name in your sick call, and you'll be reimbursed until they get rid of it."

"We're not getting rid of it," the satyr said frankly. "Do you know how much paperwork and time that thing has already saved us? Not to mention peace of mind!"

"I don't want to eat lunch twice every day," said Doris. "And it always ruins our chances of having a boss."

"Yes, exactly," said the satyr. "The perfect result."

Doris glared at him, but the miniature centaur said, "You've been doing better work since you had to decide things by yourself, haven't you? You already know what to do; you just like having someone tell you to do it. And you could say that the lunch reset was because you keep working through your lunch and the computer doesn't have a code for that."

"I should be able to work through my lunch if I want to," said the gargoyle in a small, annoyed, pebbly voice.

"Yes, but you like to tell us about it and make us feel bad for not working through our lunches when it's busy," said one of the willowy tree-women, with a bluntness belied by her soft appearance.

Doris turned a deeper grey colour and said, "Fine. I won't do it."

"The rest of us like it," the tree-woman said to Zero, with no less bluntness. "We'd rather you left it. Anyway, it's good experience for us, working with human things. When the day is going smoothly, we can even use it just like a normal computer—there are just a few extra things to it."

There was a murmur of agreement, and the centaur said, "We really would rather keep it, sir."

Zero looked around at all the tentatively hopeful faces and found himself unexpectedly touched. The group of people he had met that morning would never have trusted him with their wishes—just like he had been, they had been trained from childhood to obey their betters and perform their tasks without question. They wouldn't have dared to voice opinions of their own in any other Behindkind office.

It seemed to him that he felt the weight of that confidence almost palpably.

"I'll see what I can do," he said.

"WHAT ARE we going to say in our report, sir?"

Zero's eyebrows twitched up before he could help it. He glanced over at Palomena. "You're back to calling me *sir* again, I see."

"Yes, sir. It occurred to me," she said, with a perfectly straight face, "that given the kind of problem we had encountered, it was best to avoid giving the computer more reason to make your position untenable while we were within reach of its influence."

"I see," said Zero. He was as well aware as Palomena that the computer had had no issues with titles; it had an issue with how he performed the duties attached to that title. "As to the report, it can wait until tomorrow. I don't think the computer will do any harm to the office-workers, and they seem to know exactly what they're doing with it. It'll take some finesse to get the upper levels to understand exactly what they shouldn't do, and I don't have the mental energy for that today of all days."

"Are you saying that you think the current office setup is suitable as it is, sir?" There was a faintly incredulous note in Palomena's voice.

"Of course not," he said. "They obviously need a manager. However, they also obviously need the right kind of manager—one who works with them instead of over them, I suppose. One who knows how to take in and direct energy in the right way, if it comes to that."

The thought still made him uncomfortable, used as he was to the rigid conformity of his childhood, and after that the rigidity of his life in the enforcers; but it wasn't as though he hadn't broken away from both forms of rigidity and thoughtless obedience himself, after all.

"In that case, do you think we might take a moment to visit one of the bakeries on our way home?" suggest Palomena. "The others will appreciate it, I'm sure, and if we're not rushing back to write up a report..."

Zero opened his mouth to say something cold and off-putting, but what came out instead was a brief snort of laughter. "Get me something with strawberry in it," he said, and while Palomena started off down the footpath as if afraid that he was going to change his mind, he put a hand over his pocket, which had begun to buzz.

Zero rather bemusedly took his phone out of his pocket and stared at it. Almost nobody called him. Nobody but his niece, that was.

With something of a shock of fear, he tapped his suddenly cold finger against the answer button—once and then twice when the first tap didn't work. The call picked up, and he put the phone to his ear, his breath coming too fast.

"Yes. Speak."

"I thought you might like to know, sir," said old Leonard's voice.

When had old Leonard got himself a phone? When had he learned to use any such thing? Had Zero's niece been passing out human technology to all and sundry in the household?

Zero shook his head in bewilderment, trying to dislodge those thoughts, because what Old Leonard was saying was more important than how he had gained the knowledge of this method of speaking the words.

"Sir? Did you hear me?"

"You thought I'd like to know what?" Zero said, trying to process too much all at once. "Say it again."

"Aye, well, I thought you'd like to know, seeing how out of sorts you've been all day about it. I just got word that it's a little girl, sir. The mother is in good health, and they're waiting for you at the hospital—the human one, they say. They said they tried to call you but couldn't get through, so they left a message with me."

"Yes, good," said Zero, with relief blazing through his chest so strongly that he was surprised he could speak. "She's in good health, you said? Pet is alive and well?"

"Her and the little one are both fit as a fiddle, sir! Spoke with her myself, and she sounded much as usual, but perhaps a bit tired. They're waiting on you for the naming, I shouldn't wonder. Shall I tell them you'll be around, sir?"

"No need," Zero said, wiping at a troublesome moisture nearby his nose and catching the taste of salt through a grin that he didn't seem to need to think about, or be able to banish. "I'll go there myself directly."